BEN

A Novel by

MAX SCHOTT

1990

NORTH POINT PRESS

San Francisco

LIBRARY OF CONGRESS
CATALOGING-IN-PUBLICATION DATA
Schott, Max, 1935–
  Ben : a novel / by Max Schott.
    p.   cm.
  ISBN 0-86547-430-3
  I. Title.
PS3569.C52828B4   1990
813'.54—dc20   89-29847

To Alan Stephens

BEN

I

The manure cart had big heavy wooden wheels with wooden spokes and iron rims. I put my shoulder to the pushbar, but by myself I couldn't get the cart untracked.

I walked down the row of stalls, looking for Ben. He came around the corner of the barn, leading a horse. "It's full," I said.

"Is it? Well, then, you must've filled it, that's fine." After he tied up the horse he fished his watch up out of his pocket; he held it out as far away from himself as he could, and cocked his head. "It's a slow day," he said. Then he walked over and took hold of the pushbar of the cart with both hands and angled his long body forward to push. We shoved it along to the edge of the bank, where Ben tipped it up like a wheelbarrow and dumped it. "Now let's take ourselves a rest."

I sat down flat on the gravel with my back against the barn wall and my legs stretched out.

"Tired, son?"

I shook my head as manfully as I could.

"I am," he said, squatting down.

I wanted to say I was too, then, but it was too late.

Ben closed his eyes and stayed still, ignoring or not feeling the three or four flies that settled one at a time on his hands; but pretty soon he shook off the one that landed on his face and opened his eyes. "I never can get used to these summery winters," he said. "My brother's got a place up north—green as a garden this time of year, dry in the summer."

"A ranch?"

"Uh-huh. Up in the hills. A person can raise cattle, a few sheep, a little hay. I might go up there myself one of these days and try it, just go on up and stay put."

"Don't you like the stables?"

"No, sir, I don't. It's been good to me though, the stables has. I'll look back someday and say, 'That was all right, that stables. I put money in the bank while I was there. That's how I got where I am today.' I'd like to have somebody around to say it to, though."

"Your brother?"

He smiled. "No, I don't think him." Then he stretched and groaned, but made no move yet to get up. He looked at me as if he were thinking, or taking me into account somehow. "Thursday night—that's tomorrow."

I nodded.

"Your mom and dad, they have folks over pretty often, do they?"

"No."

"And they don't know me. Could be you might have asked them to invite me yourself. Be fine if you did."

"No, my aunt wanted to," I said.

"But I don't know her at all," he said. "I met your dad."

I nodded.

After a pause, he said: "Could she have thought your dad ought to find out a little more what I'm like, since you're spending so much time over here? Could it be something like that? Be all right if it was."

"I think so," I said.

"Well, then, that's a good reason," he said. "And your aunt, she's probably learned a little caution, in her line of work. I don't think I ever ate supper with a lawyer before. How old a woman is she?"

"She's not old at all, she's young," I said.

He gave me a long look. "I'll bet she's a particular favorite of yours, could that be?"

I blushed and nodded.

He stretched out one leg, took his billfold out of his pants pocket and opened it up. "Look here."

It was a photograph of a woman's face—young, with long hair in a single braid. "Is she your girlfriend?" I said.

"Once she was, she was once, you bet." He laughed, and looked at the picture himself.

Groaning a little, he got to his feet. I scrambled up after him. He drew his watch up out of his pocket again and held it out. "Four o'clock," he said. "You look at it, son—what's it say?"

"Four o'clock," I said.

"She might have it in her hand this minute." He looked at me as if I weren't there. "I sent her a letter." I nodded. "A grown man, trouble himself over a woman. Lot of foolishness, wouldn't you say?"

"I don't know," I said.

"No? Well, then, you're better off," he said.

When I got home my father was in his study sitting at his desk, holding a pencil. For sixty or a hundred seconds I talked—about Ben, Ben's brother's ranch, the work we'd done. He nodded and rolled the pencil in his fingers, looking into the air. "Are you doing chemistry?" I said finally.

"Am I doing chemistry? Oh, probably not. I don't know what I was doing, but now I'm listening. Tell me again." I refused at first, but he fixed his eyes on me this time and listened.

I went into the kitchen. "Ben's here." Rose looked out the kitchen window just as his car rolled into the driveway. "Should I bring him in to meet you first?" I said.

"Why, what are you thinking? He's a guest, you take him straight to your father."

When I opened the door Ben was coming slowly up the front steps bareheaded, his hat in one hand, held by the crown. His face, which he must have just scrubbed and shaved, was big and rawboned and red. His blue eyes, freed now from the shadow of his hat, were brighter or less mild. "Hello, son, good to see you."

"Fine," I said, and, blushing, led him through the house out onto the porch where I'd been sitting with my father. But my father was gone. "Would you care to sit down?" I said.

"Surely."

He sat down in one of the deck chairs, with his hat on one knee. "Say, that's some view now, isn't it."

"Thank you," I said.

"You don't see an old country boy like me here at your home too often, I imagine?"

I shook my head. "My dad is in with my mom, I guess."

"Best place to be."

"Could I take your hat?"

"Why, sure, son, if you want to. Just hang it up anywhere."

When I came back I said: "Is there anything I can get for you?"

"Me? No—getting along fine. How far would you say the ocean is from here?"

"Six miles."

"Six miles—well, I'd say that's about right. That's a big old ship, isn't it. Tanker. Looks like if you had a long arm you could reach out, put your hand in the water and pick it up."

Ben didn't move his arm though. He was nervous and contained. He sat still and symmetrical, feet flat on the floor, knees close together, elbows turned outward, forearms on the chair arms and his fingertips touching. After a minute or two he moved his right hand up to his shirt pocket and touched the cloth with his thumb, lightly at first, then pressed harder until the paper inside rustled. "Answer to mine," he said. I nodded. "Came today. Good thing, too. Not the answer I was looking for—but a person hates to wait. I do, anyhow."

"I do too," I said.

"That's right. When I was a boy, all I did was wait—that's how it seemed. 'Take a cold tater and wait'—isn't that how the song goes?"

"I don't know," I said.

"It does."

"What did you wait for?"

"Well, supper. I'd take that cold tater and wait, glad to get it sometimes. And payday—wait a long time sometimes, for that."

"Did you when you were a boy?"

"You bet, all my life. I went to work for wages before I knew what the word meant, almost, and I knew what work meant before I knew what wages meant, too." He laughed, briefly, and my father stepped out from the bedroom, down the porch. Ben got to his feet. "Doctor!" he said and began walking along in long strides. My father, coming toward him, got in only a few steps. "It's good to see you again, sir."

"I'm glad to see you too," my father said. "Please call me Myron."

"Myron," Ben said, and they shook hands.

Then Ben sat back down in the deck chair and sat still. My father sat where he'd been sitting before. The *International Logic Review* lay open, coverside up, on the arm of his chair. He turned it over in his hands, looking at it as if he'd never seen it before, or as if he didn't know he was looking at it, then closed it, laid it down on the chair arm and rested his elbow on it. He looked up at Ben.

"There's a view now," Ben said, disconcerted but trying hard, and swung his head from west to east.

My father grunted amiably.

"Don't you think so, son?" Ben said to me.

I nodded.

"Myron, I believe if I was a boy and had a home like this one, you'd have to bring in a steam derrick to move me off this porch, and especially not to go over to that stables and roll horse manure onto a flat shovel."

This was well said, but my father didn't know what to say back, and said nothing.

"Here comes Anna," I said.

"Oh?" my father said.

I pointed at her car. Ben looked too: an old yellow Buick convertible, flashy and battered, with the top down, coming up the hill; but almost all we could see of the woman herself was the red bandana on her head.

"My wife's sister," my father said.

Ben nodded.

"My wife is ill," my father said. "Would you like to meet her?"

"I'll be pleased to, Myron, surely," Ben said. "Whenever it's convenient."

My father first, then Ben, glanced down the porch at the door my father had come out of earlier.

We heard voices coming from the kitchen. "Anna's talking to Rose," I said to Ben. "She's our maid."

"That's fine, son," Ben said. "I wish I had one."

I listened again, and couldn't hear anything. "She's gone to see Mom," I said. "She'll be here in a minute."

"Oh, yes . . ." my father said. He turned to Ben. "My wife is ill."

Ben opened his mouth, nodded, and looked out over the city. "Some view."

"Thank you."

There was a pause.

"Myron," Ben said. "I believe Maxie told me you do your chemistry research in a lab downtown."

"Yes?"

"I was just wondering. . . is it where you can see it from here?"

My father laughed an explosive high-pitched little laugh. "It usually is," he said.

Ben ran his hand up through his hair.

My father followed the hand with his eyes, and stood up abruptly, his big oblivious brain startled I think by the wrong he had done. "Here," he said. "Look."

Ben got to his feet. Relieved, probably, to be in motion, he lined himself up behind my father's arm, bent his knees and sighted down it. My father pointed out a landmark, then another. The two men began estimating distances, Ben asking questions and deferring to my father whenever he could. They worked their way back through the city to the stables, which was only on the next hill over. We could see the shapes of the horses in the renthorse corral and tell that they were lined up at the manger, eating. Ben asked my father if he rode.

"In military school, long ago. I enjoyed it."

"And the military school, did you enjoy that, too, then?"

"No. No, I didn't."

"Was it your folks that—"

Through the near door my aunt stepped out onto the porch. She was pretty: thin, quick, small, young—and pretty.

"Oh," my father said. "Were you in with Kate? Ben would like to meet her."

"Would he? I'd like to meet him. I'm Anna," she said, and

shook Ben's hand. "Is there a drink in this house? Or an ashtray? Myron is rich as sin but he doesn't know the value of money."

"Don't be silly. You know you're welcome to—"

"Ben, what would you like?—There's everything here."

"There isn't, but you're certainly welcome to—"

"—everything they have. What can I bring you?"

"Oh, there's no need," Ben said. While my aunt and my father had been talking, I had seen him smile to himself. "She's here," I thought. "Now everything will be easy."

"No, no—please," my father said, turning up his palms.

"Well—bourbon and water, if you folks are having something."

She went inside, and we all looked for a moment at the door through which she'd come and gone. "Is Anna a lawyer then, like Maxie says?"

"Yes," my father said.

She handed Ben his drink, set her own down, offered him a cigarette and took one herself; she sat down, crossed one leg over the other and began swinging her foot.

"Won't bother anybody, I hope, if we smoke?" Ben said.

"Not at all," my father said.

"And yourself, doctor?"

"No, thank you."

"He doesn't have a single bad habit," my aunt said.

"Well, I admire that," Ben said. "I've got two or three I could rent out, though, if anybody's short."

"I tried to take it up once," my father said. "Smoking. I'd heard it called a nervous habit and sometimes in the evenings I'm rather nervous . . . My intentions were good but—" he shrugged and laughed.

"Here," said my aunt, holding out the pack to my father.

He shook his head.

"You see?" she said.

Ben stood up, struck a match and cupped it in his hand. She turned her face up to him. He bent down. I stared. My father glanced at them once and picked up his journal.

"Blow a smoke ring," I said to her a minute later.

She blew two, narrowing her eyes, then grinned at me, melting my heart for the thousandth time.

"How was it you happened to go to military school, again, Myron?"

"My mother thought I wasn't manly enough. She was right. We tried various remedies."

"I hope she was happy with the results," my aunt said.

"She was satisfied with her efforts. I'm not sure she was aware of any results," my father said carefully.

"That's it," Ben said, "that's it! You take a person who knows he's always in the right, you can't shake him, not if you prove him wrong fifty times you can't."

"She had a gym instructor come to the house on Saturdays to teach me to box. A very nice man—Dolly was his name. 'It's all shadowboxing for you, Myron,' he used to say." My father touched the rim of his glasses and laughed. "Once she even had me put in the hospital for a week because she thought I looked tired. She was right again, you see. I *was* tired." He laughed again and twisted around in his chair.

"Hospital?" Ben shook his head.

"How old were you?" I asked.

But he'd become distracted again and seemed to hear me through some other thought. "Oh . . . seventeen. Yes, I was seventeen." His body stopped moving. He turned to my aunt. "Don't you think we should bring Kate out now? She might enjoy it."

"She's asleep," my aunt said. "I was just in."

He got to his feet and hitched up his pants.

My aunt stood up too. "I'll go."

"No—no, please, you were just in."

"I know I was—she's asleep," my aunt said. She laughed, but wouldn't sit down.

"But I could wake her," my father said. "Ben would like to meet her."

"Ben isn't leaving, he just got here," my aunt said.

"No hurry," Ben said, "—just whatever's convenient."

My father sat back down, on the edge of his chair; my aunt sat down too. "What should we think of a man who's so fond of his wife?" she said.

"Now there's a fault the world could use a little more of," Ben said. "She'll have you sent up for being a paragon of virtue here if we don't keep an eye on her, Myron. I don't know what the penalty for that is . . . life, I guess."

My father said nothing. Then Ben fell silent too. And even my aunt was subdued. Then Ben, maybe from sheer desperation, went on: "Yes, sir, I'd try that myself if I knew how. To be fond of your wife and live with her, both at once, that's the cat's pajamas. Did you and Kate meet in college, Myron?"

"Yes, in fact, we did. Actually it's rather strange. I met Anna separately and at nearly the same time, without knowing that the two were sisters, but I often forget whom I met first—though they both tell me it was Anna."

"You went out with her first too," I said.

"Yes, that I do remember." He smiled at my aunt, who had lowered her eyes. She raised them though and smiled, with an effort.

Ben looked at her, saw she was suffering and began to talk

about how the sun was going down fast now—you could see it sink.

"Well, I wonder if Kate's awake," my father said. My aunt didn't say anything this time, and he got up. He moved slowly at first, as if he were afraid she might try again to stop him—but once beyond the circle of chairs he pointed himself toward the nearby open door and with a sudden increase in speed, went through it.

Ben smiled at my aunt. "So Myron's mother put him in the hospital . . . isn't that something now!"

She gave him back a sort of wan, grateful smile. "And where were you, Ben, when you were seventeen?"

"Well . . . between a rock and a hard place, I think."

"Where did you grow up?"

"All over, pretty much."

"You have to have started somewhere."

"Colorada—Manzanola."

"Colorado?" I said.

"Coloradah, we called it. 'Dust' for short, our part."

"Did you go to school?"

"Why, sure, son—can't you tell? Did well, too, till I quit. Wasn't much bigger than you are."

"Why did you?" my aunt said.

"I wondered that ever since. My daddy told me not to. 'You'll regret it if you quit,' he said, and I do, I regret it to this day." He looked solemn, then laughed.

I watched my aunt looking at his big open-featured face.

"But you have your law degree," he said. "A good-looking woman, she's running in the lead to start with, the way I see it. Add an education on to that, and she'll fly like an angel."

"Some people don't look at it quite so generously."

"No, but I'll bet there's plenty that do. Myron, now, I'll bet he does."

"He's different." Suddenly she blushed. She touched her collarbone with her fingers. "I should go help."

She smoothed her skirt violently as she got up. We watched her as she walked fast down the long porch toward my parents' bedroom.

Her thin ankles, the quick click of her shoes, the angry motion of her body: she was freedom personified, to me. And yet it was painful to watch her: the world was so big, it struck people down, and she looked so small—like a bird in the wind. I felt—along with the usual adoration—a kind of dumb pitying love.

"Is Anna over here at the house often?" Ben said.

"Every day almost."

"That often? You see! You're a lucky man."

"You can come over and see her too," I said.

"I thank you, son, for the thought."

Without realizing at first what caused us to, we turned again. The bedroom door was standing open. The wheelchair's small front wheels came out first; then my mother's knees, covered by a shawl.

"Mom has a tumor in her brain. It's growing," I said, brightly. To have a tumor in your brain—like a ship in a bottle—would be novelty enough alone, but to have one growing was nearly a miracle.

Ben said, after a moment: "I'm sorry to hear that."

My aunt was pushing the wheelchair. My father followed along behind. My mother's head hung forward, her chin touching or nearly touching her chest. Her head, and body too, bobbled gently with the easy motion of the chair.

Ben sat looking solemn and composed.

When the chair came to a stop my mother raised her head

to look around. Something—dizziness or a warning of pain—made her lower her head or let it sink again almost as soon as she had raised it. She closed her eyes. Ben was on his feet. "Kate—" my aunt said. My mother raised her head. "This is Ben." She smiled on one side of her mouth and moved her lips. My father looked on, smiling strangely—half-proud, half-ashamed —standing off a little to one side with his head cocked.

"I'm pleased to meet you," Ben said.

"Are you here for dinner?" my mother said, with effort and almost inaudibly.

"Yes, ma'am," he said, leaning forward. "For supper. Thank you."

"I'm Kate," she said. Then she closed her eyes and lowered her head. Ben sat down. She lifted her head again. "Is mama coming?" she said to my father.

"No, dear."

"Isn't it Thursday?"

"It is, but your mother's been dead now for some years."

"Are you sure?"

"I'm sure. It's one of the things I'm sure of."

She nodded. A look of confusion, but not surprise, passed over her face. She lowered her head and closed her eyes. A moment later she raised her head and looked around. One eye protruded, which made her look seem intense. "Are you Ben?"

"I'm Ben, Kate, yes," Ben said. "From over at the stables. We've never met before tonight."

She nodded, smiled, let her head sink and closed her eyes. She remained that way then for a long time.

The sun went down. Rose had gone home, and my aunt went into the house to get supper ready to put on. "There's Venus," I said, because that was the early, easy star. My father and Ben began to look at the sky. They knew the constellations about equally well and agreed, when it got darker, on which star was the North Star. Ben found it by "looking at the sky," my father by extending downward a line made by the bowl-edge of the Big Dipper. Ben said that was a good way, and if he was ever lost he would remember that and use it. My father laughed and said he thought he was more likely to get lost than Ben was. "You won't lose that Big Dipper, though," Ben said. My mother sat quietly without raising her head. "It's a little cool," my father said. "Don't you think so, dear? I think I'll take you in." He took hold of the wheelchair grips. She didn't answer or move, until the chair moved—then she gave a little cry, and he stopped.

"I didn't know where I was," she said. "I think I was asleep."

"I thought you were awake," he said, smiling down at her.

"I am right sometimes," she said.

"Yes, very often," he said. "But it seems to me you've slept an awfully lot today."

"As usual," she said.

"But usually when you put your head down I don't think you are asleep—are you?"

"I was. You woke me. I was startled."

"Yes, dear, I know." He patted her, and began to push the chair.

He left my mother with my aunt, came back out and sat down. "The stables keeps you busy, I suppose."

"Too busy. It's been good to me though, the stables has. I've done all right, here-lately, in that respect."

"But not in others?"

"I can't complain, Myron. Shouldn't, anyhow."

"But if you did . . ."

"Well, the truth is, I'm a married man."

My father laughed. "Oh, well, that's not so bad."

"I mean to say, she's not around."

"Ah, well, that would be bad. But do you have plans to—be together soon?"

Ben shook his head.

"At any rate, I hope you're able to—see each other occasionally?"

"She doesn't want to."

"I see. I see more clearly," my father said.

"I don't say I don't still hope though," Ben said. "I got a letter just today."

"Good news, I hope."

"No, no news, nothing new."

"But at least a letter," my father said.

"That's right, at least that," Ben said, gloomily. "It's a funny thing. If I was out and saw myself walking down the street, first thing I'd say, I'd say, 'Now there's a fella, I used to see him walking with his wife—but he looks more married now than he did then.' "

"I doubt if most people would say you look particularly married, or unmarried for that matter."

"That's right—it's only a feeling, isn't it. But when I was with her I didn't have it quite so strong—or if I did, I didn't know it. And Audrey, she doesn't have it now as strong as she did then. Might not have it at all, to hear her talk."

"Or, by the analogy you suggest, might only think she doesn't have it," my father said.

"That's right," Ben said. "I hope that's right."

"Are you hungry?" my aunt's voice said. We turned, she was standing in the doorway.

"Supper?" Ben said.

"Just about. Are you hungry?"

"Sure am. These two gentlemen, they just heard my life story."

"Really? Then I've missed something."

"I tell it over and over," Ben said.

"Ben was telling us about his wife," my father said.

"It's a sad story, Anna, I tell it to myself every night."

"I didn't know you had a wife. Will you tell me too, later?"

"That's what the women always say—later. But I will, sure. Can't forget it, might as well talk about it."

My mother's wheelchair was pulled up next to my father at the table. She had her own tray, fastened onto the chair.

My father, beginning to carve the roast, asked Ben how he liked his meat.

"Done well, if there's a choice," Ben said.

My father held up an outside slice.

"I like it just like that," Ben said.

"That looks good," my mother said.

"Why, Kate—would you like it yourself?" Ben said.

My mother shook her head. "For you," she said.

"Ah! Well, that's kindness," Ben said. "I don't know if I deserve it, but I appreciate it."

My mother smiled and nodded.

My father cut my mother's meat into small chunks. She picked them up between thumb and forefinger, one at a time quickly, ate them all almost before he could put anything else on her plate, then didn't want anything more. She lowered her head and closed her eyes. Occasionally, during the meal, she roused herself to look around. Once when she looked up at Ben and smiled at him or seemed about to say something to him, he said: "I'm married too, Kate."

"Where is she?"

"She's not here tonight. I wish she was. You'll meet her another time, I hope. Audrey's her name."

"But where is she?"

I stared: his neck had turned a bricky red.

"Well, she's way down in San Diego now, living."

My mother nodded. She put her head down and closed her eyes, and after a little while my father took her better hand in his hands and held it—but the hand jerked away in a little convulsion. He reached for it again and held it—it lay quiet. She raised her head and smiled, but only at him. "Are you tired?" he said. She nodded. "Would you like to sit with us a little longer?—or go to bed?"

"Sit with you," she said.

She lowered her head and closed her eyes. My father let go her hand. She was quiet for a time, then her body jerked and she raised her head up suddenly. "Myron?" "I'm here." He reached for her hand. "Would you put me to bed now, please."

After my aunt and I had cleared the table we went into the living room, where Ben was. She sat on the end of the couch, near Ben's chair. There was a distance between them of a few feet, but they were as close together as they could get—this was how I saw it. I sat down on the other end of the couch; far from him, necessarily, but with a big unnecessary space between me and her. To make a show of it, I turned my knees away too.

My aunt didn't mention Ben's wife until he did, but then she said: "Do you write to her?"

"Every Monday night, just like taking a pill," he said.

"Does she write to you?"

"Here's one here," he said, touching his shirt pocket. He leaned forward. His forehead glistened. He looked at my aunt.

"I have to do the dishes," I said, getting up. He looked at me without seeing me.

"Let's do them later," my aunt said.

"You don't need to help," I said, and started for the kitchen.

I could hear her coming behind me. She shut the kitchen door after us, I turned around, she put her hands on my shoulders, bent down and kissed my forehead. We went back together. She tried to hold my hand, but from embarrassment, laughing a little, I pulled free, and sat down close beside her on the couch.

"Son, if they'd chase me like that, I'd run too," Ben said.

"So you have a letter—?" my aunt said.

"Here it is," he said.

"Oh, no," she said, raising her hand before he had got it all the way out of his pocket. "I didn't mean to . . . ask to see it."

He reddened. "I didn't mean to be so forward."

"Of course you didn't. I was forward."

"Well, I will be then," he said. "Sometimes it comes easier, talking to a stranger, and maybe someday I could do the same for you. Anyway, I'd like to ask, if you don't mind. You're a woman . . . maybe you might know what she wants."

"What does she say she wants?"

"Now, today?" he said, touching the letter.

"In general, let's say."

"In this letter here, she doesn't hardly even say anything. I was hoping she would, after the letter I wrote her."

"And in other letters?"

"Same thing. She just says she likes everything the way it is, fairly well."

"But, she does answer your letters?"

"Sporadic," he said.

"Are her letters friendly, when she does write?"

"More friendly than I deserve."

"But she must not think that, since she writes them."

"I hope," he said. He sat silent a few seconds, swallowed and went on. "I drove her off. I didn't know I was, but I did. 'Talk to me,' she used to say. 'Why won't you talk to me?' I'm a hard man to live in the same house with, or I was then—she'll give you a warranty on that."

"Would you be different now?"

"I don't know if I could," he said. "I used to tell myself to be different, then. Rained a lot that winter. I was working construction at the time. Rain, I couldn't work. I'd look out the window into the yard, say to myself: 'Stop sulking. You're having hard luck, lots of people having harder luck than you.'

"And she'd come in and ask me what was wrong, and I'd say, 'You can see what's wrong, look out the window.' She'd tell me it wasn't just that, and I'd say, 'If a man can't work, what good is he?' —And she'd say, 'You can work, it will stop raining.' 'Will it? Maybe,' I'd say. If she was lucky, I'd say about that much, and if I did, if I was even that civil, she'd smile . . . breaks your heart to think about it . . . so I don't, too much."

My aunt smiled, but her mind was all lawyer-like now—or almost all. "When Audrey told you that it wasn't just that you couldn't go out to work that made you sulky, did she know what did make you that way?"

"I knew what it was, she didn't. I took something away from her, but for a long time she didn't know. I made her suffer once by taking it away, then I made her suffer again for the harm I'd done her. That's low, isn't it? Pretty low."

"What was it you took away?"

"She's a town girl. Comes from ordinary people. When she was little they couldn't have bought her a horse or even a ride on a horse. But she learned to ride, learned on borrowed horses, hanging around a riding stables in Culver City and working, like Maxie here, if he was poor. Then later, when she was a little bigger, she started to enter the bucking-horse contests in the rodeos they put on there for the kids. But it wasn't just horses, anything that'd buck they'd try—they'd ride anything: calves, sheep, cows, young bulls, wild sheep from the islands, mules, work-horses, jackasses. If they could fit it in the chute, she'd get on it; stay on it too, more often than not. She and her girlfriend, Nicky, time they were fourteen, fifteen, they had a little reputa-tion—the girls that could beat the boys.

"Then when she got to be about sixteen, people—her family and the boys and even her girlfriends—started telling her, and Nicky too, 'You're too old now, too big: this rodeo riding, it isn't ladylike or feminine.' And so they quit their bucking-horse rid-ing and learned to trick ride and Roman ride. That's what I saw when I saw her first. She and Nicky, of a Sunday they'd each strap two horses together, and race. They'd go around the track just as fast as they could make the horses run, the girls standing up, a foot on each horse, and some of the horses almost as wild as the girls. If the horses'd pull apart, they'd drop down on the back of one, or if they didn't do that quick enough, they'd have to go on and fall between the two horses and roll in the dirt, on that hard ground."

"Ooh," my aunt said.

"It's scary, isn't it, to a sensible person.

"I watched her three Sundays in a row. I thought I was watch-ing the whole show, but I like to think now I was just watching her. On the last Sunday, after the show, they put on a dance. I went, and I saw her standing off to the side and thought—I won't say all I thought. I thought she'd be as wild afoot as she was on horseback. I went up to her and said: 'I saw you ride—you can sure do that. Are you old enough to dance too?' She looked about fifteen, and I was thirty. I figured she might just say 'try me.' But she looked down and turned her head away, then turned back and looked up. 'I don't know how.'

"I didn't see what difference that made. 'Well, step right out,

I'll teach you.' But she shook her head and turned pink. I felt like a big lout then, with a big loud voice and big hands that there wasn't anywhere to put. And she turned away, and walked away. And that's the story . . . I don't know. Is that the story I started out to tell?"

"But she did take to you eventually."

"She did, didn't she. And I was the luckiest man in the world, I thought. I thought so then, and I see it now for a true fact."

"What happened next?" I said.

"Son—? Too many things. Anyhow, we kept company awhile before we married. And her riding buddy, Nicky, she married in that time—and quit riding.

"I remember I said to Audrey, 'That's a shame. Now you have to do it alone.' And when I heard myself say it, I realized I wanted her to quit too."

"Why?" my aunt said.

"Yes, sir—why?" Ben said. "Then we married too. And married people are different—or I was: she found that out. She was twenty and I was thirty-two—she looked up to me like a god. But I cured her of that. It was hard, but I did.

"We rented a house in Gardena. Lots of people kept a horse in their yards there, sometimes two or three—still do. She had her own good little trick-riding horse by then, but he crippled himself, as horses will. She didn't want to sell him at first—thought he might get well. I said, 'We can't afford to feed two.' So she quit riding for a little while. It's always for a little while, you know. It was hard to ride there anyhow, almost in town. And without Nicky it was hard. She needed encouragement, but I gave her discouragement. Before that, before her horse went lame—this is what I should have told you: she'd wanted to go off, take her horse and go to a rodeo. It had been their dream, hers and Nicky's, to go on the road—and it still was hers. So maybe somebody'd see her there, at the rodeo, and give her a chance to try out, stock contractor maybe, maybe he'd hire her, for a contract act. It was just a pipe dream to her; she didn't believe in it, herself, because she didn't know how good she was. But I did. And even aside from that, just to see her go off alone, without a protector, when I had to stay home and work . . . But she didn't go. I made it hard."

"Did she need a protector?"

"No, but what if she found out she didn't need one, you see?" He paused, my aunt looked alert and waited. "And I'll tell you another worse thing, about myself. What if she found out how good she was? What if they did hire her?" Again my aunt said nothing. "She might tour the world, probably could if she wanted to, and what would I do? Carry her currycomb? She was all potential, and I didn't want her to know it. It's a shameful thing: I was ashamed, but it only made me mean."

"And she—did she do nothing about it?"

"She changed. She started to change, or we all thought she had. She put on a few pounds, looked even better for it, learned to cook—fairly well. Her folks were pleased to see her settle down. She hardly went out of the house even. Nowhere to go much anyway. She sketched more than she had before—she always liked to draw. And she never had talked much, but she got quieter. I'd clipped her wings."

"What a pity," my aunt said.

"What a pity!" Ben said. "I could talk faster and sulk harder than she could, and bit by bit . . . Well, anyhow, I never thought she'd leave. If I'd thought that . . . I misjudged her there. When she was sad she blamed herself, gave back good for bad. She'd ask me what was wrong, and I'd say: 'Nothing's wrong, with you.'

" 'I feel like there is,' she'd say.

" 'Then maybe there is. You're after me all the time, maybe that's what it is.'

"And she wouldn't say anything. Or maybe one word: regret.

"And I'd say, 'If you regret getting in you can always get out.'

" 'You know that isn't what I meant.'

" 'Don't tell me what I know.' There wasn't a kind word in me to say, or if there was I'd put a twist on it and it was unkind when it hit the air. I was worse every day. She'd start to cry, go off somewhere, bathroom usually, and I'd sit there thinking, thinking about myself. 'She knows me now.' But she didn't know me yet. In the bedroom on the bureau she kept a photograph I'd given her, in a little stand-up frame.

"I said to her one morning when I saw her looking at it, 'You're tired of looking at that.'

" 'I'm not,' she said.

" 'You looked at it long enough,' I told her. 'What do you want to have to look at it anymore for?'

" 'I *don't* have to,' she said."

"A photograph of—?" my aunt said.

"Me, me myself. 'You're tired of it,' I told her, and turned it around.

"She turned it back around. 'Don't!' she said, just like that: 'Don't!' She's just no more than a girl, you see.

"I turned it around again and she turned it back again. 'It's mine,' she said. And I took and pulled the picture out of the frame and tore it up, with her looking on. She didn't say anything, just bit her lip, tears running on down her face. She went out and didn't come back till almost dark. 'I'm going to leave,' she said, soon as she walked in the door. I remember right where I was standing. Funny thing is, it took me by surprise.

"I said: 'Don't go.' I started talking about her horse, right off.

She must've wondered why. I wondered why myself. I said, 'Let's get another one. We can keep two. We'll borrow some money. People borrow to buy a car, we'll borrow to buy a horse. Then you can get outside more, like you used to.'

"'I hate you now, because you're cruel.' Like a child she said it. 'I hate you now, because you're cruel.' I wasn't man enough to be her helpmate, so I had to make her mine. But then I couldn't stand that, either."

"And, would it be different next time?"

"It's always different next time," Ben said.

"Would you still wish she'd stay at home, in the house?"

"Oh . . . I guess I would, I'd wish it."

"Hopes are cruel," my aunt said.

Ben bowed his head.

"I didn't mean just yours." She leaned a little toward him.

"Do you have a picture of her, that we could see?"

"Only picture I carry."

He took out his billfold. My aunt and I looked together. "Looks just as good the second time, doesn't she, son," Ben said. Then he looked himself, shook his head and put his billfold back in his pocket. "After the letter I wrote her, I guess I kind of had my hopes up."

"Was it a good letter?"

"Guess not."

"Were you serious when you said you write every Monday?"

"Monday night, whether I want to or not. Say about the same thing, too, every time."

"And do you call?"

"Way last spring was the last time."

"The last time?"

"There was somebody there—a man. Hit me pretty hard at the time. But I'll try again if you think that's the ticket."

"Do you think there's still 'somebody there'?"

"I don't think so, right now."

"When you write you usually say the same thing, but last time you wrote you didn't say the same thing. . . Do you mind my asking questions?"

"I want you to. You can be my lawyer, anytime."

"What do you say, usually, when you write?"

"Oh . . . 'How are you? I'm doing all right up here myself. Business is good, been good all week. I put some money aside, same as usual. Bachelor life, it's pretty quiet still. Getting by all right, getting used to it. I hope you're all right down there. You say you are, and that's always good news. Brother Clyde, he hasn't written me back yet from the north, but I guess he's all right—usually is.' I'll go on like that. Never wrote a love letter; never wrote one, never got one—maybe I don't know what one is.

"And she'll write me back about the same way, little different sometimes. She'll say she likes it down there pretty well still, likes being on her own, making her own way, has a job in a store and she doesn't like that, but she likes having it and drawing a salary, for now, while she sorts herself out. Sometimes she'll say she still doesn't know for certain what she wants, but whenever I need the divorce to just write and say so and we'll still be friends. I'm the best friend she has—she says that sometimes, said it once anyhow. And she'll say she's glad we can still talk and be friendly even if it's only by mail and she likes my letters and she's sorry we both had to get hurt, but as time goes by it can only get easier and better—things her mother told her, probably—and I'll write back and say, 'yes, it's better now,' and she'll write and say, 'yes, now it's better.'

"But then she sent me a letter—I got it a week ago tomorrow. I read it through and read it again, couldn't keep it in my pocket, kept taking it out, put it in a drawer finally and went downtown, ate a steak and went dancing—had a fair time—had to come home though, and when I come home it's still there in the drawer. She'd gone out with a friend, she said, said it was a man-friend, said she didn't want me to feel there was anything now she couldn't tell me—she said there had been, but there wasn't now. Fired me up inside, I don't know why. And I figured I'd better not write right then the way I felt. I waited all through the week-end, pretty busy then anyway. Woke up Monday: 'I'll write,' I thought, 'I'm all right now, no use to feel bad when she meant to make me feel good.' "

"Could she have also meant to make you jealous?"

"I don't know, Anna, I hope so."

"What did you write?"

"I wanted her, I said, and she must know I did and I didn't want to hear about any men or man for any reason, because it was her business, but it was like sticking a knife into me and turning it. I said I wanted her back and when she left it was my fault and I'd try to make it up to her if I ever could, but I couldn't from here and if she didn't want to let me I wouldn't blame her but I couldn't take much more of this the way it is now, even if—" his voice broke and came back husky "—if not to ever see her again was the last opposite thing to what I wanted and always had wanted. 'But if you still do have some feeling for me,' I said, 'the way I think sometimes maybe you do, and if you still do need more time, just say so and I'll wait. I won't mind waiting,' I said, 'I'm just upset.' And here's the answer." He cleared his throat and reached into his shirt pocket. "Would you mind looking at it?"

"No, I wouldn't mind."

"Doesn't say anything hardly at all, but it's got a picture on it." Then he turned to me, though he only took his eyes off my aunt's face for an instant. "Son, I'll bet you think that's enough crying the blues for one evening." I shook my head. "You'd be about right if you did. Read it out, Anna."

" 'Dear Ben: I didn't mean you to be upset. I'll try to explain someday. Look, I drew a picture (see over). Love, Audrey.' "

It was a pencil drawing of a girl with a long braid who had one arm around the neck of a donkey, mostly you saw their two big faces close together; and under the donkey, written in pencil: Male Friend. My aunt and I looked at it together and she laughed.

"Some joke I'll say, after the letter I wrote her," Ben said.

"Is it a real donkey?"

"I bought him for her two years ago, to keep her from wanting to go back to her horse."

My aunt smiled.

"Not good for much—just a pet. She didn't take much of an interest in him, at first."

"She seems to like him now."

"Yep," Ben said, still ruefully. "She teaches him tricks," he added, almost with contempt.

"And she definitely likes you."

"Me?"

"Your letter may have come too soon for her to quite know how to respond to it."

"Too soon?—It's been a year, it's been more than a year."

My aunt said something again about surprise, about the difference between his last letter and the other letters, then stopped, her own face soft and flushed, and looked at his face: he wasn't listening. "Too soon," he said, and nodded his head slowly. "Maybe so. I hope so. I'll remember that, a man ought to write that on his sleeve: too soon." He looked up. My father came into the room. "I hope Kate's resting well, Myron."

After Ben had gone, we washed the dishes, my aunt, my father and I, quietly enough. (My father tried to show us that it was better to rinse a dish twice with a little water than once with a lot.) Then I went to bed, and falling asleep, in a kind of dream I saw her face. She moved her lips to speak, and I could almost touch them. But then she lowered her eyes, her chin sank, and it was my mother. I woke up. There were voices in the hall, my father and aunt. "Good night," she said, in a strange dull voice. "See you tomorrow. You don't need to see me out."

"Anna—?"

"What?"

"We ask an awful lot of you. Tomorrow Rose and I can easily—"

"You don't ask anything."

"No, of course, because you always offer, but, I mean to say, I . . . Kate and I would like to somehow make it clear to you just how much we—"

"Do you know that you are very often very foolish?" she said, with a bitter little laugh.

"Yes, of course," he said. "And I know you don't wish or expect gratitude but—"

"Shhh. Stop, please. You are a good kind man, but please don't feel grateful to me—please."

He was silent then. I heard the door close, and through the window I heard her crossing the asphalt; every sound she made I lay still to hear, until she had driven away.

II

Late on a Friday afternoon, a few weeks after Ben's visit, my aunt stopped my father and me as we came into the house—before we could go our separate ways. She wanted to tell us "part of a secret," she said. "Ben was here this afternoon."

"Oh? To see me?" my father said.

"No, me," I said.

"He came to thank me," she said, looking a little smug.

"What for?"

"For saying he should call his wife."

"That's rather obvious advice to receive, I should think—even from an attorney." He laughed at his own joke. She made a face. He raised his eyebrows. "—Besides which, I should have thought he would have thanked you at the time the advice was given."

"He did."

"Then why should he thank you again now?—or today, for example, rather than yesterday or tomorrow?—that's the question."

"But I'm not going to answer it," she said.

"Did something good happen?" I said.

She looked at me, poker-faced. But I didn't laugh. "I don't

care. If you won't tell me, I don't care. I'm going to see him tonight anyway. We're going to the auction."

"I know," she said, and that was all she would say.

My father sat in his chair near the bed, reading. My mother lay on
her back awake, her head raised by the pillows. I came in and
said: "It's time to go."

"To go? Oh, yes." He turned to my mother. "I'm going to give
Max a ride over to the stables. He's going to the auction with
Ben. Rose will come in and sit with you." She nodded. "But I
think Mom would like you to take a jacket," he said, smiling at
her. She looked at me and nodded.

"I don't need one," I said. "It's not cold. Let's go, it's late."

"It's not cold now," he said, raising his eyebrows and looking
again at my mother. But her eyes had closed.

I went up closer to the bed. "Goodbye, Mom."

"Goodbye, dear," she said, opening her eyes.

We went out.

I could feel my father watching me as if he were going to say
something. I thought I knew what it was about and tried to put it
out of my mind. I had been impatient. When we were in the car
I almost did put it out of my mind. "Can we go up the up-is-down
hill?"

"We could," he said, giving me a sly look, "if it weren't so late."

"It's not late," I said. "Ben said six."

He didn't answer. He stopped at the bottom, with the hill rising in front of us, turned off the ignition and put the car in neu-
tral.

"Can I steer?"

"Probably you can. You certainly may."

The car began to move, rolling slowly, then a little faster.

"We're going up," I said—as I always did.

"It appears so, at any rate," my father said, joining in.

"We don't usually go this slow," I said.

"Patience is strange, isn't it?" he said. "Or impatience, perhaps I should say, the way it comes and goes."

"Why?"

"Oh, I don't know, shifts in our attention I suppose."

"I should be nicer to Mom, is that what you're going to say?"

We came to what looked like the crest of the hill, went over, and went on, rolling a little faster down the other side. "*Should* I say that?"

I shook my head.

"It's rather tempting to blame people for their own illnesses, especially if—"

"I don't."

"No, we can't really, can we. She has us stymied in that respect. It's not what . . . she would have wished. Ben says you work hard."

I nodded.

"I'm not able to work. I make myself useful, but I don't work. I have work on my desk, I have at least the illusion that I even have it in my mind ready to be done—yet I don't seem to be able to do it, or at any rate I *don't* do it."

I nodded.

"Work would be a great comfort, I should think."

We started up the stables hill, which was a real hill, curved and steep. I'd gone with Ben to the horse auction last week too, and the week before that. Each time we'd taken two of the rent horses: Strip and King, Lady and Kate Smith; tonight it would be Sonny and Banjo. He was selling them all off. He was going to leave. Two weeks ago he had even taken a trip, to look for a ranch, and come back happy and secretive. I felt his excitement, made it my own, and luckily hadn't foresight enough to feel my own probable loss. We came to the top, the road leveled out, we could see the barnyard and the barns and the pipe hitchrail where Sonny and Banjo were standing tied, ready to load, and Ben's trailer, already hitched up to his car.

He'd heard us coming, and came walking down to the dirt lot to greet my father. They shook hands. "Come on in," he said. "We have a few minutes. Will you drink some coffee? Come on in anyhow, if you have time."

"I'll drink some," I said.

"You will if your dad says you will is what you'd better say now."

My father laughed and shrugged and said he didn't mind if I drank coffee as long as he didn't have to.

We followed Ben over to the ramshackle little house, which had been hauled here by the landlord from somewhere else and set down on the hillside away from the good level ground reserved for the riding ring and the barns. We went into the kitchen. That was where Ben mostly lived: a clean, square little room with a butane stove, an old icebox, and a table covered by a shiny yellow oilcloth. On the table were some broken bridles laid out on pieces of newspaper, and an open pocketknife, a leatherpunch, a small riveting machine, two or three kinds of awls and chisels, some scraps of leather and rawhide, a can of neat's-foot oil . . . After he'd turned the fire on under the coffee, Ben pulled the newspaper with all these things on it to one side and said: "This is home, for now. It's kind of a boar's nest, the way I keep it."

"It's pleasant," my father said.

Ben laughed and said, "Well, you'd make a good bachelor then, Myron."

"I'm afraid I wouldn't, actually."

"No, and I don't either. But my exile's about to end, I hope."

"You mean . . . ?"

"Her mind's made up—if she doesn't change it."

"Why, that's wonderful. But, is she *going* to change it?"

"Well . . ." Ben reached out and knocked on the wood wall with his knuckles. "No," he said, and shook his head. "She said to me just yesterday: 'You're a married man.' And I said to her: 'I have been for a long time. What's your situation?' And she told me. Right here in this room." He looked around, pointed at an empty chair, as if it weren't empty, and laughed.

"When will you see her next?" my father said.

"She's gone down to San Diego to break the news to her folks. I tried to talk her into coming up again tonight, to take in the auction, maybe look for a horse . . . But tomorrow night anyhow, we're going out dancing."

"They met at a dance."

"You remembered that, son. Yes, sir—three years ago. I went home that night, and couldn't stop seeing her face. Saw it the next night, too. I'm still seeing it. I was a free man, up to then."

Ben didn't seem as nervous as he had at our house, and my father was more comfortable too. I sipped the bitter hot strong coffee, taking it black, like Ben.

My father smiled and said: "Not many married men are as eager to go dancing with their wives as you are—so we are led to believe, at any rate."

"That's what they say in the song, isn't it?—" Ben said. " '—I saw a man, he danced with his wife.' "

"Yes, they do," my father said, and after a moment of dreamy or just absent-minded silence looked at his watch. "Oh, my," he said, stretched and rose. Ben got up too. "Can I show you something, before you go?—just take a minute."

"Of course."

And they both sat down again. Ben took an envelope out of his shirt pocket. "You know I went north. This came today. The real estate agent sent it to me, along with some papers. I forgot he even had a camera."

My father took the snapshot and looked at it. "Ah, you didn't go alone! Very good."

Ben and Audrey were sitting close together on an old swing-couch on the gallery of an old low weathered-looking house, behind which you could see a grassy hillside and part of a barn. She was looking down, Ben was taking a bite out of an apple.

"Is it your brother's ranch?" I said.

"No, son, this one's ours, the lease on it is. Papers came today."

My father congratulated him, then said he was sorry, for my sake especially, that Ben was leaving. Ben reached over and rubbed the top of my head with his knuckles—scrobbed my knob, as he put it. "I'll need help," he said, "all summer long, if you folks can spare him and he wants to come."

"I do," I said.

"Wages wouldn't be much, but you're used to that. There'd be cows to chouse and at least one to milk, hay to put up, a river to swim in—though that's not mandatory. Be a big help, to me. It's something to think over—no hurry."

"I don't need to—I've thought it over," I said.

"Your dad might need to. We old folks think slow, got more to think about."

But my father said it was fine.

"Well, we settled that. There's one more thing, Myron, before you go . . . it's what I've been leading up to, in a way. Does Kate travel well?—ride all right, I mean, in the car?"

"Kate? Why, yes—so far at least."

"I know a person hates to tempt fate—"

"Oh, I doubt if fate is very often tempted."

"Then you don't mind if we talk a little into the future, about your own plans?"

My father shook his head.

"I talked to Anna this afternoon, I called her, down at her office, and then I went to see her, at your house . . . "

My father nodded.

"Well, you see, around Easter time, when school's out, if Kate's still traveling well, I wondered—I'll tell you the truth, I called Anna to see if she thought you'd mind being asked and she said, 'No, I think it's a wonderful idea'—those are her words, Myron, so you see you've got her to blame, too . . . I wondered if you might all like to come up and pay us a visit? Anna, Rose too if you'd like to bring her. It should still be green up there then, and I'm a pretty fair kind of a cook."

My father was taken aback. "Oh, my, that's—" and he started to say how much trouble we would be. But Ben stopped him, partly by sweeping his hand through the air to brush aside all objections, mostly by a flow of speech. "No, no, we don't mind trouble of that kind. There's four big bedrooms in the house, and there's a bunkhouse too—you can't see that in the picture. And there's light and heat and running water: carbide lamps and a butane stove, wood stove too. Gravity water, coming down from the spring. The pipes run along the top of the ground, so on a good sunny day, at the end of it, you can draw a warm bath. And there's an icebox, no worse than this one, and ice for sale eight miles down the road—I mention it in case there's medicines or things like that we'll want to keep cool. I believe we could find everything we need, one way or the other. Audrey thought so too. There's a lot to consider on your side, I know that. The apple orchard makes a good shade—if Kate likes to sit outdoors."

"She does."

"Well, you see then?"

"I see," my father said, smiling, and started again to protest—but Ben wouldn't let him.

"You go home and talk it over with Kate, and Anna too."

My father hesitated, then, "All right, I will."

Ben walked with him back down to his car, and I tagged along. The sun had set, but it was still light.

"It's quite a step I'm taking," Ben said, "—broad jump, don't know where I'll land. Anna says, be sure it's not too soon. I've been thinking that over. Trouble is, if you're sure it's not too soon, it might be too late. Isn't that so?"

My father laughed and said that almost everything is so. He was about to open the car door. Ben turned his head, stopped moving and held up his hand. We stood still and listened. A car was coming. We heard it hesitate, downshift on the hill, and come on.

"It's her," Ben said.

She pulled up into the lot. We could see her face sticking up not very far over the steering wheel. It was smooth and round, and she wore her hair in a single long braid—the way she did in the photographs.

Ben walked fast over to her car. We watched her get out. She was small and slender, like my aunt but more surefooted and more shy, and in the twilight, quick and bright. He went up close and touched her shoulder. She reached up and touched his face. She glanced at us. Then they kissed. My father put his hand on my shoulder and asked if we shouldn't let them be alone together tonight. She ducked her head in below Ben's chin and pressed the side of her face against his chest, as if she were hiding from us and even from him. Then she put her arms all the way around his back and hugged him hard.

"You mean, and me not go to the sale?"

"That's what I mean."

Ben brought her over. When he introduced her to my father she said, "I'm very glad to meet you," in a voice you could hardly hear, and looked down. But she said "Hi" to me easily, and when my father asked Ben if he could speak to him a moment, she said, "Come on, let's go look at the horses."

We went over to the hitchrail, while Ben and my father walked toward the barn. She asked me Sonny and Banjo's names, how I liked working for Ben, and said he'd told her about me. "Well, they're going to talk," she said, glancing back. So we walked across the barnyard to the renthorse corral. She picked up an old hemp lariat from the fence and shook it. It was limber from having hung coiled up so long in the sun. She tossed the loop over the top of a post, backed up twenty-five or so feet to the end of the rope and with a flick of her hand threw a sort of curl that traveled like a wave down the rope and flipped over onto the post—a half hitch. She did the same thing again, then walked up and pulled the half hitches off and said, "You try!"

I tried a few times from up close, and did it once. "Good," she said. She didn't know that my evening's fate was in the balance. Under the eaves of the barn, where the gathering dusk was thickest, Ben and my father were still talking. I could see the outline of Ben's face. He nodded while my father spoke. Then Ben spoke, then he was silent, and then he nodded again. He didn't shake his head once: that was bad. "Match you!" she said. "Best out of ten."

She took her turns left-handed and missed some. I was almost going to win, I thought, when Ben said, "Son—?"

I met him at the hitchrail. My father stood back, waiting patiently to take me home. She stayed where she was, too. With her right hand she threw—Ben stopped to watch—a double one, or anyway two single ones in a row so close together that they seemed to travel down the rope at the same time. I tried not to look directly at Ben, but he looked hard at me. We could hear the rope slap the post every time she threw a half hitch.

"I told your dad, if you didn't get to come along tonight, it might be quite a disappointment."

"No," I said, shaking my head. The rope had stopped. She was too far away to hear what we said, but she was watching.

"But there'll be other times," he said.

"I know," I said. The corners of my mouth turned down. She flicked the loop off the post and started toward us, coiling up the dragging rope neatly and quickly along the way. "It's okay," I said to Ben.

"What is?" she said.

Ben said something quietly to her and she said, "Oh, no. That's what I thought. No, no." She pulled on his arm.

My father had come walking over too. "Pardon us," Ben said. "We're going to have to confer." She was pulling on his sleeve.

He followed her around to the other side of the horse trailer. Through the plexiglass window, which made their faces look distorted and strange, I could see him tilt his head to listen.

Below the trailer tongue we could see their feet, her small ones in moccasins, unmoving, while he scuffled the toe of his boot back and forth, raising puffs of dust. We could hear her voice, soft and insistent.

My father was interested now; he was paying strict attention. "How adamant she is!" he said. "You'll have to go now whether you want to or not."

Ben's boot toe came to a stop. "You're right," he said at last, in a deep voice.

After my father'd driven away and we'd loaded the horses, I started to get in the backseat of the car.

"You sit up here with us," Ben said. "We'll put Audrey in the middle, so she won't get away."

"I don't want to get away," she said.

"That's our best hope in the end," he said. "There's a blanket in back. On the way home you can curl up under it if you want to, son. Be late, then."

On the way we drove through the neighborhood she'd grown up in. When we passed her old house, Ben slowed down. When we passed Sunset Stables he came almost to a stop. A couple of dim bulbs along the outside wall of a long barn only made the night darker, to me. But Ben and Audrey saw things as they used to be, or at least, saw the things that used to be there. "Do you remember . . . ?" he said. "Yes," she said, and after a minute, "Do you remember . . . ?" Yes, he remembered too: as if the days before they were married were long ago but had come alive in a new way in their minds. As we drove along, I looked at her face. It was round and symmetrical and smooth—not a mask—what she felt at any moment passed over it—she was quick to smile or frown, and would make faces for fun, and laugh. Yet thought or suffering had left her face less marked really than the face of a child. Everyone was struck by it, though we didn't know what it was we were struck by—we simply looked. But it was not her, but the urgency of Ben's own feelings that attracted me most. She was there to be won over, by him. Then he would be happy; and she would too, as a corollary . . . He reached over and put his hand on her thigh; she moved close to him and put her hand on top of his. That's good, I thought, and looked away.

Sonny and Banjo were city horses. Bright lights, traffic, crowds, and noise were nothing new to them. Even so, they opened their eyes wide and picked their feet up higher than usual as we led them across the big graveled lot, toward the bright open door of the auction barn. The silhouettes of others like ourselves (though mostly men) crossed the lot in the same direction, converging. The gravel under our feet—and the horses' feet especially—made a lively sound, and when we got closer I could hear the electric, staticky sound of a microphone, then the hum of voices—masculine. She drifted against him as we walked; he put his arm around her.

At the door we paused. It was for people to go in, not horses. I heard the auctioneer say: "They're wet behind the ears, boys, but we all were once."

They were only selling baby calves, Ben said, so we had lots of time before any horses would sell. "Let's look around out back. Might find just what you want, on a night like this."

"What kind of night is this?" she said.

"Just a night," he said, "—to some people." And she nestled up to him again.

So we walked around back to the stockyards. At a gate, a man took Sonny and Banjo from Ben, asked him how gentle they were and how old, and gave him a receipt. It didn't take long. Then we walked up a cleated ramp. Another man, old and small, wearing glasses, was sitting in a little open-air office—like a corral with a desk, except it was raised and had boards for a floor instead of dirt—he looked up at Ben and recognized him. "Webber?"

"Yes, sir. 'Evening," Ben said.

"You can buy yourself a whole trainload of horses tonight."

"Be about a thousand too many," Ben said. "I'm selling these days. Are they good ones?"

"They were good once."

They both laughed, like a ritual. "Is Jerry around?" Ben said.

"He is, somewhere."

"We'll find him then."

We walked along the catwalk looking for Jerry, who was a horse trader, and looking down, as we walked, at the horses that had been good once. There *were* a thousand, I thought. They were everywhere around us; come by rail, Ben said, from big ranches in Texas and Oklahoma, where there was a drought, to be sold by the pound to the meat-packing plants, for dog food, because there was no market anywhere for so many saddle horses. We passed over pen after pen of their thin backs and their necks and ears. The bays and browns were dark in the dark, while the duns and grays and a few pintos and roans threw back the lamp-light and stood out, though even they were dull and rough-haired.

Then in a pen by himself we saw a horse colorful enough to draw the attention of a crowd or an audience. He was a reddish color, but there must have been silvery hairs mixed in, to make his red coat shine, and he had white stockings and a wide blaze of white on his face, and a flaxen mane and tail. "Well, now!" Ben said. We climbed down into the corral. "Well-made horse, too, wouldn't you say?" She nodded, and let herself be absorbed, looking. Ben slapped his own leg, to scare the horse. He ran a lit-tle way, then turned and faced us, ears thrown forward, eyes big. "He's sound, I believe," Ben said.

She did not say anything. She and I stood back.

Ben, with old, practiced, deliberate caution walked up to the horse, spoke to him, stroked his neck once or twice, ran his hand along the side of the jaw and rolled back the upper lip with his thumb. "Good young horse," Ben said. "Five-year-old." He stepped away to look carefully at the horse's legs, then stepped up to him again, again slow and deliberate and cautious, and ran his hands down along the shoulder, over the knee, the whole length of the leg, feeling each joint and flat place, to the hoof—then the other leg, then the hind legs. "Sound, I believe," he said again, stepping back.

"Wait," she said, and came forward, not with caution but grace, as if she were another horse, or had lived with horses in a field. She ran her hand down the horse's left front leg like Ben had—but at the knee she stopped, felt of it, pinched it, and when the horse stood unflinching, pinched again, hard. The horse didn't move. Then Ben came up too, and they found a needlemark under the hair.

I thought the horse was beautiful, and was disappointed. Ben was disappointed too—his face got long and he was silent, but she laughed and kidded him about being gloomy about nothing, and when he saw how she was, he was all right too. The walkway made a turn. The bright and noisy auction barn, dome shaped, was right beside us. I smelled, as a single odor, living horses and cattle and dung and wet straw and shavings and maybe gasoline or exhaust, and at the same time, as another single thing, chili and coffee and frying grease, anyhow food. But we turned the other way, still up on the catwalk, and began to pass again over the shadowy long rows of fences and gates. "There's your friend," she said.

Ben and I looked. Just below us, a man wearing a baseball cap and a neckerchief and chaps and with a bulge in his cheek (that was tobacco) was sitting on a horse in a corral full of horses. The horse he was on stood perfectly still, and the man, too, looked almost asleep, while the loose horses milled around slowly. Maybe he was studying them, the way she had studied the other one.

He didn't look up at us, though he must have heard our feet on the boards almost over his head. "There the old bastard is, all right," Ben said in a loud voice.

Jerry slowly turned his head. He had a square prizefighter-looking face, but it seemed to change when he recognized Ben and opened his mouth. He had a gold tooth, too, which flashed in the dark.

"And with the missus," he said, touching his cap. "Some fellas have all the luck—always the ugly ones too. I never could figure that. Come on down here. Let's get in the next pen. Too much dog meat in this one."

He had a gate to go through. The horse—a red sorrel like the other one—stepped sideways to the gate. Jerry put his hand out and took hold of the latchbar. After that, he didn't move in the saddle, he didn't even move his arm. The horse did the moving: first stepped backwards—that freed the latch—then stepped sideways to pull the gate open, then pivoted around the end of the open gate (staying close to it all the while so that the man's hand never had to leave the latchbar), then stepped sideways in the other direction to push the gate shut from the other side, then stepped forward to send the latch home again. It was like a dance between the horse and the gate, with the man pretending not to be in it. This horse had a white blaze too, and socks, and soft big luminous eyes, which looked sleepy.

We climbed down into the pen. Ben introduced me as "the foreman." Jerry said: "You need one. Keep him in line, son."

"No, no," Ben said. "He's the foreman, but I'm the boss."

I grinned and didn't say anything.

"Well, what are you looking for?" Jerry said to Ben. And to Audrey: "I never see him unless he's looking for something." And to me: "I've got a monkey at home. You want to buy a monkey?"

I shook my head.

"A horse," Ben said.

"I've got fifty-four, last count, and a bucket of paint. Make you anything you want. Can you be more specific?"

"We're looking for something we can make a trick-riding horse out of," Ben said, trying to sound as casual as Jerry did, but it was too important—he was talking for her, and his voice was tense.

"I saw one down here in a pen. Not mine. Man brought him in this afternoon. Colorful horse, lots of color."

"More novocaine in him than a dentist's office," Ben said.

"The hell there is? Well, you should have come to me, you see. Ought to always deal with a man you know."

"I'm trying to," Ben said. "What's this here?"

"This horse here? He's mine."

"I figured that. Is he for sale?"

"I never had one that wasn't, you know that."

"Well why don't you try to sell him to us, then."

"I am. You know what the man said about the mule. They asked him: 'How come you brag on all your mules but that one?' 'Don't need to brag on him, he brags on himself.'" Jerry laughed, picked up a few strands of manehair and tugged on it. The horse opened his eyes wide and backed up five or six steps rapidly, then came forward to the same spot and stood without moving, eyes half-closed as if he were half-asleep.

"He's too old though, I imagine, for what we want," Ben said.

"Does he look it?"

"I didn't say he looked it."

"Precocious," Jerry said.

"What's his name?" Audrey said.

"Just whatever you want to call him."

"What do you call him?"

"Me? Pay Window."

"I'll bet you just thought of it," she said.

"That was a good little chestnut horse I used to see you ride," he said.

"He sure was, thanks," she said.

"She's been afoot a long time now," Ben said, solemn again. "Too long."

"Except for a donkey," she said. But this passed unheard, or anyway went unanswered. Ben looked gloomy, and Audrey turned after a moment to climb the fence.

Ben followed her with his eyes. She sat on the top board, her heels hooked on a board lower down, elbows on her knees. Her face was up as high as the pole lamp, which cast its light down so you couldn't see her expression, or weren't sure of it. It was as if she'd removed herself a little, making things more complicated now—as we all dimly understood, in different ways.

Jerry saw his sale in danger of stalling. He bit down on his chew, not to swallow it. An instant later the horse sprang forward running, ran three or four strides, clamped his tail, dropped down on his hocks and slid, spraying gravel against the fence and our legs. The horse crouched on his hind legs, spun to the left, spun to the right, centered himself and started running backwards, knees lifted high. Jerry, clicking a little with his lips, stopped, slouched in the saddle, let the reins go slack—and the horse stopped and stood, flanks heaving.

Jerry stepped off, stood resting with his hand on the horse's neck. "Get on, try him out for size," he said, to the space or gap between Ben and Audrey.

Ben waited for Audrey to answer. She didn't.

He looked up at her. Her face was out of the light and turned a little to the side. "Audrey will," he said. She didn't answer or move. He walked up to her bravely then, and, speaking softly, touched her knee. She relented, and came down.

The horse was still Jerry's, to her, but she rode him around, at a walk, and sat on him a little longer after that, to please Ben—and when he asked her if she would like to go with him to Jerry's tomorrow "to quarrel over a price," she agreed to. We were all glad, Ben especially—and he told Jerry about the ranch.

"You old son of a bitch!" Jerry said. He spat, for emphasis, and became completely serious in manner, or thoughtful. "I envy you."

"Well, old son," Ben said. "—Sell out. Sell your horses—like I did. Sell your place, you old rich bastard."

"Horses aren't worth much. Market's low," Jerry said.

"It's low for me too. You don't envy me that," Ben said.

But Jerry only shook his head. They'd come to an impasse of temperament: Ben's clarity of purpose—Jerry's common sense.

When I asked Ben if Sonny and Banjo would sell to the meat packers and be killed, he said: "Could be, son. Maybe not. Wouldn't usually. Might tonight."

We went in. The auction barn was full of legs, hats, smoke, craggy faces, voices overwhelmed by the one magnified voice repeating numbers so fast that I couldn't make out even what the numbers were, let alone what they meant. We found seats on a bench high up.

The thin horses from the Texas and Oklahoma ranches sold in lots of a dozen or more at a time. Driven into the ring by men on horseback carrying whips, frightened and weak, dazed by the lights and noise, the horses made for every likely exit, knocking into each other as they ran from gate to gate, sometimes ramming their faces into the fence cables, which in the bright light and confusion they couldn't see. "You can read their life stories on their hides," Ben said. "See the brands?"

No lot of this kind—selling by weight for meat—was kept in the ring long. After calling out a stream of numbers—of which I could only understand the first and last, and taking three or four bids from men in the front row, the auctioneer (sitting up high above the ring on the far side, two women next to him busily writing) called out: "Sold, Kal-Kan, one nickel," or "Sold, Skippy, four and a half cents!" Per pound, as I eventually figured out—which meant forty-five or fifty dollars for a thousand-pound horse. Then a man, positioned behind a chest-high wooden barricade, jerked a rope: a gate opened; the horses, seeing a way out, ran onto the scale; the swaying floor terrified them, but jammed against each other facing one way as they were, they couldn't turn around to escape back the way they had come—and the gate closed. The scale rocked and creaked. I could see the weighmaster above it, sitting in a booth, looking through his glasses at the balance arm and slowly, calmly shifting the pieces of metal.

The fact that these horses had come here, with a history of hard, exotic work, to die, was also part of a romance—for me, though I would not quite say so even to myself. It felt good to pity them, and to hope for the salvation of Sonny and Banjo.

The younger, fatter horses, mostly local, if they were rideable and weren't obviously lame, came through the ring one at a time, shown by a rider, and were sold by the head, not by the pound. Even so, many of them too were bought by the meat packers, when no one else would bid.

Some of these horses were ridden in by a man who worked for the auction yard, some by a boy who helped him. The ones ridden by the boy sold best, probably not because of him, but I thought it was. He was hardly bigger than me, but a better rider and more confident and experienced and tougher. The auctioneer would say: "Here's one, folks! Gentle for a child to ride. Look at that!"

Pretty soon he came through the gate on Sonny, riding him bareback, with just a halter on his head, getting him to maneuver better than I ever could, and after that, sliding off over Sonny's

hind legs, and even crawling under his belly in a showy, quick
way, to show how absolutely gentle Sonny was. So Sonny sold for
seventy dollars, to a riding-stable operator, and Banjo did too,
with the boy riding. He had saved them, I thought. And I felt
small, ungrateful and mean.

Ben was relieved, though his mind was mostly on other
things. He and Audrey were sitting close together. They talked
in low voices, as you almost had to during the auction, and
laughed. I was tired, the bench was hard. The voice I didn't want
to hear and couldn't understand was loud, the voices I wanted to
hear were too soft. The boy, and worse than him, my own jeal-
ousy, had made me feel lousy. I pitied myself. There was little
pleasure in that. But before long Ben tapped me and said, "Pie?"

In the cafe, which was in kind of a big lean-to built onto the
auction barn, the woman who waited on us was an old busy-
body—so I decided anyway, and when I asked for coffee, like
Ben, to go with my pie, she looked at me, then at Audrey, ignoring Ben altogether, and she waited, without writing it down.

"Do you like milk?" Audrey said to me.

"Sure. Milk," I said, blushing, but not sorry to have milk instead of coffee.

"He can have coffee, though, if he wants it," Ben said, looking pretty fiercely at the waitress. She looked back at him more
fiercely, and Audrey looked at him too, trying to keep from
laughing.

"I don't say he *should*, I say he *can*," Ben said. "And his dad says
so too, if you want to think about that." And he looked the waitress right in the eye.

"That's all right. Milk," I said.

The waitress shook her head wearily, in disgust, wrote it down
and turned away.

"She'll eat you alive," Audrey said, laughing. "You'd better
watch out for her."

"She'd better watch out for me," Ben said.

"Still, you don't want to stay awake all night," Audrey said to me.

"It's fine," I said.

"It won't keep you awake, if you don't think it will," Ben said.

"Coffee kept me awake, lots of times, when I didn't think it would," Audrey said.

"You weren't much of a thinker then, if you couldn't learn from experience," Ben said.

"I'm a slow learner, like you," she said, made a face, and punched him.

They were silly and argumentative, and I was part of it. That made me feel good, and happy. But I couldn't keep from yawning.

"See? He needed that coffee," Ben said.

I lay down on the backseat under the blanket. When the car started moving I closed my eyes. We moved along through the city streets. When we stopped I would open my eyes, afraid sometimes that we might already be home. Once at a traffic light I saw them kiss on the lips, his big square-cornered face, her small smooth, round one. They were almost unaware of me now. But that was all right. I didn't lose the feeling of connection.

She hardly talked, but Ben talked. "I think about my daddy sometimes," he said. "He never had much—a little dryland farm—had it almost paid for, by the time he died. Left my mom a place to live, that's about all. 'My name's good,' he used to say. He meant he had good credit, all over Alamosa County. 'My name's good.' He took a lot of pride in that. More than a person should, I used to think. I'm more like him than I knew. But that's all right, he was a pretty good man, I guess, all told." His voice got husky. "That's a good horse of Jerry's. You like him?"

I could see her head nod.

"We won't go wrong this time, will we?"

She shook her head.

Then they talked about the ranch, naming big complex things—rain, grass, the hills, the bank, heifers, sheep, hay, barns, working money and other kinds of money—as if they were all only the simple working parts of a single vision. And in my own mind, while they talked, I saw the old house that was in the photograph, and the big hundred-year-old grapevine growing up the oak tree, the couch-swing and the barn and the waterpipe that lay on top of the ground in the sun. I fell asleep.

When they left me off at home it was way past midnight. But my aunt's car was in the driveway.

I opened the door and walked down the hall. The door to my parents' bedroom was open. My aunt was sitting on the edge of the bed, sitting still. It flashed through my mind that my mother was dead, but when I stepped into the room I heard my father's voice—not the words but the sound, cheerful and practical—coming from the bathroom, and I heard water running in the tub. "We had a scare," my aunt said.

"Is Mom okay?"

"Yes. Now." She patted the bed and I sat beside her. "We had such a struggle. Kate had convulsions."

"You're white," I said.

"Am I?" She smiled at me. "Did you have a good time tonight?"

"Were you scared?" I said.

"I sure was, but I'm always the first to be frightened when anything happens. I'm a coward."

"No, you're not. Do you think you will sleep okay?"

She turned toward me. "Will I?" she said. "Yes—I think Kate will too."

Her face was so near, so lovely and sad, I put my hand out and touched it, then drew my hand back quickly.

She pinkened, and asked me if I wanted to help her finish getting the bed ready for my mother.

III

We were here.

It had taken my aunt and Rose together to persuade my father. They said to him, among other things, that the country air would be good for my mother, while to each other they said the change of scene would be good for him.

"Are those your sheep?" I asked.

"I admit it," Ben said.

"They say my name," I said.

"They do? How so?"

"MAAAx," my father said.

"Ah, that's it," Ben said. "I wondered who it was they made me think of. You'll be hearing a lot of that. We weaned some lambs a few days back. Those are their mothers."

"It's lovely here," my aunt said, stretching her arms up, then turning her head one way and the other. We were all tired of riding in the car. "You said it would be green, but I had no idea . . . And so many trees! I was sure Myron was going to hit one before we got here."

"There was none in the road," my father said.

Ben laughed and said: "You must be sober, Myron. When you've had a drink those trees will jump in front of your car, especially at night. Should we walk on up to the house? I'll bet Kate's ready." He walked over to the car window and bent down. "Hello, Kate." She raised her head and lowered it.

While my father was starting to help my mother, my aunt turned to Ben. "It will be nice to meet Audrey."

There was a pause. "Audrey's up the hill, at the spring," Ben said. He looked up the hill himself and pointed. "She'll come back down, before long. She'll be pleased to see you folks. We've been looking forward to this for a long time."

My father set the wheelchair by the open car door and locked its brakes. He crouched down and took my mother's calves in his hands and lifted her legs and helped her turn her body so that her feet hung just over the ground. Then he stood up and reached in and lifted her under the arms. "All right, dear," he said. She came up on her feet with a little groan. He swiveled her neatly and let her down into the chair.

Then he smiled, looked around, yawned, and pointed. "Is that the outhouse? We brought a commode, but—shall we try it, Kate?" He bent over, near to her face, pointed again. "Look."

My mother nodded. He wheeled her off through the grass. "The spirit of adventure," my aunt said, laughing.

We had all looked away (Ben looking again up the hill), when my mother gave a little cry. We turned quickly. The chair had stopped, but it was upright. She had got frightened going over a rough place, he was leaning down to comfort her. Then they went on.

Ben was worried and said he should have sent them by the path, which came up from the house. "They'll be fine," my aunt said. "Kate is like a little child now. She scares easily, and recovers easily. This is all enormously kind of you."

"I hope so," he said. "Are you hungry?"

"Oh, no, we ate in the town."

"Jacksonville? You didn't eat much if you ate there. This

place'll make you hungry again pretty quick, does me. Audrey, sometimes she'll forget to eat. She likes my cooking though, says so anyhow."

"I'll eat," I said.

But he was looking up the hill.

"Did she go up to the spring for water?" my aunt said.

"Well, no—we've got a pipe for that. She'll be coming on down, I hope, in a little bit." He looked over at the outhouse, where the chair was sitting empty now. "Myron and Kate have come to harbor. Would you like to go on into the house, Anna? We could put the coffeepot on. What was it you said, son?"

"I'll eat," I said.

"We'll see to that, you bet."

"Tell me something," my aunt said. "Do you think Audrey would mind if I walked up to the spring and introduced myself?"

He glanced up the hill, then turned and looked at my aunt. "That'd be a relief to me," he said. "I don't think she'd mind, no. But maybe you ought to take her about half by surprise, then you might catch her. Let me tell you a little more. Then you can make up your own mind, what to do." He stopped. My aunt looked at him all attention, but didn't say anything, so he went on. "Audrey upset herself, you see. She didn't mean any harm by it, none in the world. . . We heard the car coming, her eyes started to fill . . . she didn't want anybody to see that . . . so she took off . . . and when she takes off, she goes to the spring, more often than not—that's the story, far as I know it."

"But, can you say why?"

"I don't know why," he said. "She says she won't know what to say—says she won't have anything to say to anybody. But she'll come back down when her eyes are dry . . . so if you'd rather come on in to the house, wouldn't anybody blame you. We'll coffee you up."

"I'd like a walk," she said.

"Ah, bless you then," he said, and the ridge between his eyes with its two vertical creases smoothed itself out.

He told her how to get almost to the spring by following the waterpipe. "And then you'll see it there down below you. It's a pretty place. You'll see a willow clump, and below that, a trough. But, on second thought, give her a warning. When you start down, holler. I don't think she'll break and run. She might, but I don't think she will."

We watched her climb past the cabin where she and I would stay. When she was almost lost to us under the trees, Ben turned to me and said: "What did you like best along the road, son? Did you get tired of riding in the car?"

"We saw a truck in the water," I said.

"You saw one ford the river, did you. That's a sight, you bet. The bridge is too light for a big truck. Well, what do you think of this place, now that you're here?"

"What's that for?" I said, pointing to a big empty thing like a cart with big wooden wheels.

"Why, that's a haywagon," he said. "In three weeks, two maybe if it stays this warm, we're going to start to cut the meadows. We've got four big barns and we're going to fill them all, I hope, with meadow hay."

"How do you pull it?" I said.

He laughed. "Did you think we were going to have to hitch up to that ourselves and pull it, like we had to shove that old manure cart? It's a team of horses pulls this. We'll see them tomorrow. They'll pull that wagon anywhere you ask them to, full or empty."

"Are they yours?"

"Bank owns an interest in them, but they're mine, mine to do what I want with—mine and Audrey's. Shall we carry some things in out of the car?"

The old frame house lay at the bottom of the hill. Coming up nearly to the kitchen door was a garden orchard. With her head cast back and tilted to one side, my mother dozed there, the late afternoon sun behind her, while Ben, my father and I unloaded our bags from the car.

The rooms we went through first, as we came into the house, were dark, after the sunlight, but my parents' room, big, almost bare, and cleanswept, with no rugs or curtains, was light. I walked over to the window. Outside, between the house and the green rising slope, was a space of muddy dirt clotted with ruts and tire- and wheel-tracks, with bright spikes of new grass growing up out of them. A little way up the hill I could see the same cabin. And under an oak tree I saw some sheep standing together in a bunch. They were the mothers of the lambs, I thought, but they weren't calling for them. Maybe it was too hot. They were thin and shorn. Behind me, I could hear my father apologizing, half-jokingly, for the amount of luggage.

"It's best to have what you need," Ben said. "Should we put some of these medicines in the icebox?"

"Please, eventually, thank you."

"Is there anything else?" Ben said, "—as far as what we might need, or what you might need to know about?"

"I'm sure there is, but at the moment I can't think of what."

"It'll come to you. There always is something else, isn't there?—caring for a sick person."

"One hopes so, at any rate," my father said with a little laugh, mirthless. "We'll be imposing a great deal on your washing facilities too, I'm afraid."

"Fire and water," Ben said. "We've got lots of both."

"There is one thing," my father said.

I thought it would be about the sheets and tried not to listen. Out the window, under the tree, the ewes were huddled like football players. You couldn't see their heads; it looked as if they didn't have any. Their flanks went in and out. Because they were naked of wool, you could see just how they breathed, and how fragile they were. "At home I bathe Kate every morning. If that's inconvenient . . ."

"I'll put a bucket on the stove in the mornings early," Ben said. "I have a fire built then anyway—and when you're ready for it, we'll fill the tub. Couldn't pick a better time."

Did sheep always look thin, I wondered, when they were shorn?

"Oh, good," my father said. "Speaking of which—time, I mean"—I could feel him pause to look at his watch, then he went on talking half to himself—"Should I bring Kate in now? She likes to be outdoors but she gets chilled rather easily—I suppose it's still quite warm out though, isn't it?"

"Hasn't cooled off to speak of yet," Ben said. "That reminds me of something too." He lifted down a blanket from a shelf high in the closet. "Might as well put this on while we're here. Let's tuck it in, then it'll be there."

My father began to talk. I knew now it was coming. I had turned, and now I turned away again, to the window. There was no use putting the blanket on now, he said, because he would have to remake the bed, with the rubber liner he had brought to go underneath the sheets. I turned around and tried to interrupt. "Why are the sheep thin?" I said.

"What's that, son?"

"Why are the sheep thin?"

"Up there? Those sheep are the mothers. They turn their flesh to milk and give it to the lambs."

"Kate occasionally wets the bed," my father said.

I expected some catastrophe to follow. But Ben was unsurprised. "Then let's put the liner on," he said, and began pulling off all the blankets. "I'm a fair hand at making a bed." (My father pulled a rubber liner out of his suitcase.) "My mom gave up on ever having a girl, when she saw me. I was the last—four boys. So she taught me how to anchor a sheet; gave me a lot of practice, too, after I learnt. Anna'll be coming down pretty quick now."

"Oh? Is she gone?"

"Yes, sir. She walked up the hill to see if she could find Audrey."

"Audrey? Oh—Audrey, of course. Forgive me."

Ben's eyes flicked when my father said "Audrey?" but he said, "Nothing to forgive, that's perfectly fine."

They finished tucking in the blankets and stood up. As if he were about to make a speech, my father cleared his throat. "I'm very forgetful," he said.

"Aw, it's no matter." Ben put his hand on my father's shoulder and rocked him a little on his feet. "None at all."

Squirrels came in and went out through the cabin windows, even when they were closed, Ben said. And if we didn't keep the doors latched when we weren't there, he said the ewes might come in too, looking for their lambs.

The cabin was a good-sized room partly divided by an upright sheet of plywood, on each side of which was a bed.

Ben began to sweep. I began to sweep beside him—and when he stopped, I stopped too. He was standing at the window.

"That's a look I haven't seen for a while, on somebody's face," he said, and put a finger to his lips.

The two women didn't see us. Their hands and lips were moving. They stopped walking, looked past the cabin toward the house, then started again, walking slowly.

Ben stepped back away from the window and asked me in a whisper if I'd go out for him and tell them that we had seen them coming and that they didn't need to hurry in if they didn't want to because everything was under control and everybody was happy.

"Hi!" Audrey said.

"We were just coming in," my aunt said.

When I told them what Ben said, Audrey said, "Oh, good. Let's go see the donkey. You come too." She seemed eager and animated or even excited. We all walked quickly through the grass over the rough soft ground. I could see the barn ahead through the trees and hear the lambs. "But when you lose your balance, isn't it terribly dangerous?" my aunt said.

"Uh-uh," Audrey said. "Because you just drop down onto the back of one horse, before it's too late."

Standing under one of the trees in the green grass, fat and too full to eat, quietly switching his tail, was the sorrel horse. "Look, there's Jerry," Audrey said to me. "Where?" I said. "Right there," she said, laughing. "That's what we named him."

"Before it's too late?" my aunt said. "What happens after it's too late?"

"You just fall off."

"Where?"

"Oh, between the horses, sometimes. They try not to step on you—they don't like squishy things under their feet." She stopped and tossed her head. Her braid swung; her face was full of color. Even to me, she seemed too suddenly happy.

"Well, that's fortunate. Imagine," my aunt said to me, "Audrey goes racing over these hills riding two gigantic horses, standing up. But she's shy."

"I stay on the wagon tracks mostly. Or any kind of dirt roads. Anyway, I don't do it very often. Ben doesn't like to watch me . . . It's so good to have somebody to talk to," she added. "I only talk to Ben. I didn't even know I *could* talk. I can't very well."

"Are there any neighbors?" my aunt said.

"It doesn't look like it, but there is—*are*, I mean—people. But they all know each other, and I don't know them."

"You will, though."

"They're so settled. Ben says he'd forgotten what 'settled' meant till he came here. Look, even the barn is settled. You have to duck to go through the door. It's dark too. Watch out. Step down."

We went into the barn, passed through the dark and out another door into a corral. The donkey was alone there, idly nuzzling some straws on the ground. He flicked an ear toward us but didn't raise his head. Through the fence in the next corral I could see seven or eight lambs. It was true: their mothers on the hillside were thin, but they were fat and lively and trotted away to the far side when they saw us.

"Only I'm not settled," Audrey said. "Would you like to see him do a trick? You have to say yes. Then we'll start dinner, if Ben hasn't, cooking it, I mean. Ben says if I say 'dinner,' people will come at noon. Supper. I told him I'll never invite anyone anyway."

"Did he know the trick when you got him?" I said.

"No. He's smart, though. Watch."

"Why will you never invite anyone?" my aunt said.

"I will. I'm just afraid to."

She leaned against the donkey's shoulder and rested her forearm on his back. He raised his head and she said into his ear: "Do you like to be ridden the right way?"

He nodded his head up and down in big swings.

"Do you like to be ridden the wrong way?"

He shook his head no in jerky unequal strokes. "That's harder for him to do. Do you see where I'm touching him? Look. That's what makes him do it." She was pressing a spot just in front of his withers with her thumb. "Those aren't the tricks I'm going to show you though. Watch." In one motion she swung up onto his back.

Nudged in the ribs by her heels, the donkey walked around the corral one step at a time, twitching his ears. The lambs had come back now. Maybe they were curious. Between the fenceboards I could see their faces. She let him stop, then lifted her legs and spun around so that she was sitting on him backwards, facing his tail. "Don't you like being ridden backwards?" she said. He shook his head. (This time I saw her move her hand.) "Well, you can't do anything about it, can you?" He nodded. "You can? What?" She touched his loins with her fingers. He kicked high in the air, the lambs all ran away again, her mouth fell open and she flew off laughing and landed on her feet. My aunt jumped away, frightened and laughing too. The donkey stood still.

After supper, while we were still at the table, Ben said, "Should we move into the front room?"

"Oh, out on the gallery," Audrey said.

"If Kate won't be bothered by the cold," Ben said.

"Oh. Then in the front room, yes," Audrey said.

"Would you like to sit out on the gallery, dear?" my father said.

My mother said, "Yes, I would, thank you."

"Kate's head is clearer tonight," my father said.

"Yes, it is," she said, and everyone was pleased.

While my father went to get her shawl, Ben asked: "Think I can operate this chair, Kate?"

"Yes, I think so," she said, smiling up at him, then nodding.

It was almost dark. The gallery side of the house faced away from the hill and barns. A drifting slope, thick with grass, ran down to the road. Beyond the road was a low valley, solid now with the black-looking tops of trees, and beyond that, another hill, broad and unimposing: in this light it could have been a cloud. I walked a few feet into the grass and, feeling afraid, came back. My mother put her head down and closed her eyes, then looked up and said suddenly: "Is Myron here?"

"He's here," Ben said. "He went to get your shawl, he'll be right back. It's warm though tonight, almost as warm as the day. Hear the frogs, Kate?"

"Yes, I do," she said, calm again.

My father put the shawl over her shoulders. The gallery was lined with straight-backed chairs. He and Ben sat down. We could hear Audrey's and my aunt's voices in the kitchen. They had stayed in to wash the dishes. Ben sat still listening. I sat down next to him. We could hear my aunt laugh, then Audrey laughed.

"Audrey's been missing having somebody to talk to."

"It helps," my mother said, though Ben had not really been talking to her.

"You bet it does," he said, leaning forward toward her, she spoke so softly.

"Yes. Kate talks a good deal with Anna and Rose," my father said.

"They talk a good deal with me," my mother said.

"Yes, that *is* what I mean," he said.

"I usually do know what you mean," she said.

"Often better than I do myself," he said.

"Kate's hard to slip anything over on tonight," Ben said.

"She always has been," my father said.

Ben laughed and said: "You spent a lot of time trying, though, Myron."

"No, he didn't," my mother said.

"That's right, Kate, that's what I mean, too," Ben said. "Kate and I, we were just remarking on the frogs. Makes quite a chorus, doesn't it."

"Is there a stream nearby?" my father asked.

"Half a mile, but these are in the grass. I remember back home, years so dry you wouldn't hear a frog, not even in the springtime—if there was any springtime."

"Are you reminded of your old home often here?"

"Shouldn't be. That was flat country, flat and dry. I used to wonder sometimes how a human being ever came to move in there in the first place. Hot and dry in the summer, cold in the winter and dry. They say this country can get dry too, but at least it gets wet first."

Audrey and my aunt came out, and my aunt sat down—in the chair next to mine. "Howdy, folks," she said.

"That's the way to talk, you bet," Ben said.

Audrey stood behind Ben's chair. She put a hand on his shoulder. He put his hand on hers and pressed it. "Shall I light the lamps?" he said.

"Just some of them," she said.

"How many?"

"I don't know. You decide."

He got up and laughed softly. "You see? She says 'some' and I say 'how many?' You can see who's boss."

"You may talk yourself into a corner," my aunt said.

"I always do, Anna. I talk my way in, and sometimes she'll chastise me a little before she lets me come back out. And that's how I like it best."

"Shush," Audrey said.

"You see?" he said. "I'll light the lamps."

I watched Ben scratch the leg of his jeans hard with a match. It flared, he cupped his hands and carried the tiny flame to the first lamp. He turned the little lampcock: there was a hiss of gas and then with a sucking sound the bigger flame leapt up. He lit the next lamp with the same match, then shook it out quickly.

"Are your parents still living, Ben?" my father said. He pulled his chair up close to my mother and turned the wheelchair so that she could see us all easily whenever she looked up.

"My mother is," he said. "It was a poor country, but we weren't so poor. I might have made it sound that way, but we weren't, the way some folks around were. I remember one time, I was nine, ten years old—there, that's enough light to see in the dark by— I went to town on a Saturday morning with my folks. We were going up the post office steps, and I saw a neighbor boy coming down, with my own old patched-over shoes on. That was a little charity work of my mom's she'd never told me about. Funny thing is, I wanted to knock him down and take those shoes off his feet."

Ben sat down again next to me. Audrey sat near him on the other side. She put her hand on his knee. My aunt put her hand on my neck for a moment. "Was he smaller than you?" I said.

"I think he was; but my dad wasn't, and he'd have switched me fair. I didn't know much, but I knew that."

"What would he hit you with?"

"Oh, a willow stick, son, nothing fancy. But he'd had quite a bit of practice with it, by that time."

"What did you do bad?"

"Oh . . . things—me and my brothers. Wouldn't even be worth hearing, most of it. But it made the tears come, that little switch did. 'I won't cry. I won't cry.' I used to say that to myself and be crying while I said it."

"Was your father very mean?"

"Well, no, he had a mean switch, but he was a good man, my dad. It took me a long time to learn to say so. He did right by my

mom, far as he could. Took him his whole life, but he left her the
farm, free and clear . . . My mom, she was a town girl. It must
have been hard at first, ranch life, for her, but she took to it."

"What would have happened if she didn't?" my aunt said.

"She just would have been unhappy. That was the choice, you
see: do it and like it, or just do it. Those were hard times, for
women. I hate to see them pass, though."

"No, you don't," Audrey said.

"The boss says I don't," he said.

He put his hand on her hand again.

Everyone was quiet, the frogs were loud.

"Is your mother here?" my mother said.

"Whose, Kate?" my father said.

"His."

"Not here. She's in Colorado," Ben said. "She stays in town
now, little country town, knows everybody. Two of the boys,
they're still there, so she's all right. I'll put a call through, ask her
how she is: 'Oh, I'm fat and slick,' she'll say. I get a kick out of
her."

"Myron?"

"Yes, Kate."

"Have you called your mother?"

"Not for a number of years. She hasn't been alive."

"I remember."

"Yes, you remember quickly, but you forget sometimes when
you're tired. Besides, there's no phone here."

"Where are we?"

"Ben's ranch."

"Is Max here?"

"Yes, he is."

"Here I am," I said, got up and stood in front of her.

"Here you are," she said, smiled and nodded.

I had the impulse to move toward her and touch her, along with the more familiar one not to, and stood there, stuck.

My father understood and took pity on me. "Kate, do you remember the song" (I backed away and sat down), "how does it go . . . ? 'Hello, Central, give me Heaven—I know my mother's there.'"

"I remember," she said. "But is your mother there?"

My father laughed, we all did.

My mother smiled and nodded, lowered her head and closed her eyes.

"Are you sleepy? Would you like me to take you in?"

"I don't know," she said.

"It's pleasant here, isn't it," he said.

"Right now it's loud."

"What is?"

She shook her head.

"Is it gone?"

"It's gone, whatever it is," she said. "I'm sleepy."

"Would you like me to take you in?"

"Or would you like me to take you in?" my aunt said.

"So many offers," my mother said, smiling. "I'd like to take myself in."

My aunt lifted up my mother's shawl, away from the wheels.

"Is there a bed?" my mother asked.

"A fine bed, all made," my father said.

"Good night, Kate," Ben and Audrey said.

"Good night," I said.

"Good night, I'm going to bed now," she said cheerfully, and my aunt released the brake and wheeled her into the house.

"Has Kate always had such a good disposition?" Ben asked.

"Yes, she always has."

The carbide lamps started to flicker—Audrey noticed it first. I went out around the side of the house with Ben. A round white tank six or eight feet across stuck up a little way out of the ground. "Jump up and down on it," Ben said. "If there's some pellets left, that'll stir up the gas."

The lid of the tank buckled up and down under my feet like the lid of a flour tin. I jumped hard, it was fun, and the noise bounced back off the hills. In my mind's eye the lights were already burning again, bright and steady, and when we walked back around the corner of the house, they really were. "Son, you're as good as a light switch," Ben said.

Audrey was alone on the gallery. "You sit down and keep us company," Ben said to me. He sat beside her. "Kate asked for Myron," she said.

"It's a load to bear up under," Ben said.

"For everyone in the family," Audrey said.

"Yes," Ben said.

"It's impossible to feel her pain," Audrey said. "And *not* to feel it must be painful, for everyone. I'd run away."

"You only think you would," my aunt said from the doorway.

"I'm *afraid* I would."

Ben looked as if he were about to speak, but didn't.

We sat in silence for a little while. "Low on pellets," Ben said when the lights flickered.

My aunt laughed and said: "Well, I'll take it as a sign that it's time for me to go to bed. How about you? Are you coming?"

"Sure," I said.

"Come on in the kitchen, I'll light you a lantern to take up," Ben said.

"I'll say good night," Audrey said.

"Good night."

"Good night."

When Ben held the match to the lantern wick my aunt stepped back, but when she saw how gently it burned she moved closer.

I looked up at her face. The flame of the lantern was in her eye. When she blinked, it went away and came back. Then Ben put on the lantern glass.

He walked out with us. We stopped at the wire fence. His big serious ruddy face looked down at her. "Every time we see each other, you do me a good turn," he said. "I don't know how I'll get even." He held up the wire and held the lantern, then handed it across to her, and we walked through the dark by ourselves. The lantern swung in her hand, making the trees' shadows and the trees themselves move from place to place. Outside the cabin we stopped. "Just think—yesterday we were at home," she said, "and now we're in somebody else's world. I like it. Do you?" I said yes and she said: "What do you like best so far? Besides seeing Ben."

"When I jumped on the tank and made the lights come on."

"I heard you! Like God: Let there be light. I'm sleepy, are you?"

"Sure."

We went inside. "Where shall we put the lantern?"

"On your side," I said. "On the table. So you can see."

"That's nice of you."

"No, it isn't. I don't need to see. I can see in the dark."

She smiled. "Well then, good night," she said.

I could hear her feet moving on the floor as she undressed or looked through her things. I got into bed; when she got into bed, my bed moved; and when she moved in the bed, I could hear the sheets rustle.

I climbed up on the fence to look at the lambs—and saw Audrey sitting on the next fence over, looking at the donkey.

She turned. I jumped down—the lambs bumped each other running away—and walked toward her.

"Are you training him?"

"No, just sitting on the fence. Want to help?"

I climbed up beside her. "Are you thinking?"

"It's easier than thinking. I just try to imagine what it's like to be him. I can't, but it's easy to try."

We sat on the fence. I kept politely quiet; but time passed very slowly. He was small, had rough hair, long ears, small not very bright eyes, a potbelly; was slow to move: he only stood there, in the shade of the barn overhang, once in a while switching his tail or twitching an ear, and even that he did slowly, though I knew he could move fast. Once he shook his whole head, because of the flies, and once he blinked—in a slow way, too, as if he had sleep in his eyes. He was static to me and soulless, because I wasn't good at imagining. The fenceboard felt hard. Finally I climbed down.

"See you," she said, interrupting herself easily to smile at me.

Higher up on the hillside Anna and Audrey walked out from under the trees. Ben stopped work and leaned on his shovel. I did the same. My father went on digging at first. It was strange to see him working at all. The women looked over at us and waved. Ben waved. I waved. My father let the digging bar stand in the posthole and waved too. They started walking again, coming down near us but not to us. "Quite-a-looking pair of women, wouldn't you say so, son?" I think Ben was hoping my father would feel left out and stop and look too—at Anna in particular—but he picked up his bar again instead.

As they came even with us on their way down, I heard my aunt say: ". . . lost—and the donkey shows you the way?" and Audrey say: "Yeah, because . . . a lot of stories are about that, so a lot of people would understand it, without words. But should I be a lost boy or a lost girl?" "It will be easier for you to be a girl," my aunt said, and they walked on. We couldn't hear the words but we could hear the voices, and they often laughed, moving slowly, stopping sometimes, heading always toward my mother, who was parked in the orchard at the bottom of the hill, reading.

Ben began to dig again, but stopped almost as soon as he started. "Anna sneaks up on a person."

My father, making fun, stopped and looked over his shoulder. "Where?"

"You know what I mean, Myron. She doesn't wear her heart on her sleeve."

"It would be rather unsanitary."

Ben didn't laugh. "I'm on to you," he said. "You won't slip by me this time. I mean, Anna draws people to her—does me, and I never saw Audrey take to anybody the way she has to her."

I dug the loosened dirt out of the hole with my shovel. My father began digging again with the bar, loosening more dirt. But Ben kept on: "Hard to see how she does it," he said. "Doesn't seem to take any effort. Never pushes herself forward. But you've had a chance to know her now for a long time."

"Yes, a long time. Longer than I've known Kate." They both stopped working and looked down the hill. "Anna was seventeen, and seventeen was very young, compared to nineteen— Kate was nineteen, and I was twenty-one. I remember feeling quite strongly that Anna was young. I divided the world in that way then, as strange as it seems to me now . . . How still Kate sits. She looks so peaceful, reading."

The other two women walked up to my mother, under the trees.

"Yes, sir, she does look peaceful," Ben said.

My aunt bent over to say something to my mother and to touch her, while Audrey stood back. Then she went forward too, bent down and spoke. Then Audrey and Anna climbed the wood steps to the kitchen. When they went in, the screen door closed behind them.

"They're there, then they're gone," Ben said. "Well, back to work. It cures what ails you."

"Which is?"

"Work, I say—cures what ails you better than whiskey: harder to run out of." He stood leaning on the shovel, though.

"But, does something ail you?" my father said, attentive now, and gentle.

"Oh . . . sometimes I'd like to take her and put her in my pocket. I'd treat her right, give her everything she wanted."

"Unless she wanted to get out of your pocket."

"Aw, she wouldn't want that, would she? I'm just daydreaming though, you know that."

"One could say that your daydream has come true, for me, oddly enough."

"For you?"

"You see Kate, how content she looks . . . and she is content, I believe, at the moment . . . and she certainly can't go anywhere . . . and I feel quite responsible . . . even for her contentment."

"But is there pleasure in it, then, for you?"

"Sometimes."

That night out on the gallery when we were all together again, Ben said: "I don't think I ever heard you say three words in a row about your law work, Anna."

"She never talks about herself at all," Audrey said.

"Tell us, for example, what you do when you first go to your office in the morning," my father said. "What's your routine?"

My aunt laughed. "You see, Myron isn't interested, and Kate's falling asleep. Are you asleep, Kate?"

"No," my mother said, raising up.

"You looked so peaceful today reading. But your glasses slip down on your nose. Myron has to find a way to fix them."

"Yes, I did put a chain on them," my father said. "I thought that would help. Let me see." Hanging on the back of the wheelchair was my mother's purse. He found the glasses and held them up, with the loop of the chain swinging.

"It just gets tangled in her hair. The chain just gets tangled in your hair, Kate," my aunt said.

My father moved away to stand under one of the lamps. "I don't mind," my mother said. "I don't feel it." Her face pinkened—from being the center of attention it seemed at first. Then she said something inaudible.

My aunt got up and crouched beside the wheelchair so that her face was close to my mother's. "What is it?" she said, and my mother whispered something in her ear.

"That was long ago," my aunt said, and she pinkened too.

"Not so long," my mother said.

"Very long," my aunt said. "You forget how long ago things were."

"What is it?" my father said.

"Come here, dear," my mother said.

"No, don't," my aunt said. "Stay away."

"Let's finish up in the kitchen," Audrey said quietly to Ben, and they slipped into the house.

"Kate, no," my aunt said. "Don't say anything to him, please. Myron, go away."

"Where shall I go?" my father said, turning up his hands, and he went into the house too.

I sat still, hoping not to be noticed.

"No, Kate," my aunt said, shaking her head hard. "You have a generous soul, but don't, please don't."

My mother said something again that I couldn't hear, and my aunt said: "Promise. Can you remember?"

My mother nodded.

Ben came to the door and motioned to me. "Give us a hand, son," he said.

I went into the house. When I turned to look back, my aunt was still kneeling, with both hands on my mother's arm.

"Anna. Anna, it's me, Audrey . . ."

"Au-drey?" said my aunt's voice, husky with sleep.

"Me, Audrey. I'm sorry to wake you. It's . . ."

"Here. Come in. Sit on the bed. Is it morning? My God, it is, sort of. Is Ben up too? Wrap this around you. Aren't you cold?"

"Yes. Not very. I . . . all last night I—couldn't sleep. I usually can but I—couldn't stop thinking. I tried to, but . . ."

"Can you tell me?"

"I don't know exactly. I—there's Ben coming back, he won't know where I am."

I sat up and looked out one of the windows. In the half-light Ben was coming back from the barn, walking bent-kneed through the pale wet grass, a milk bucket swinging from each hand.

"Are you not happy here, with Ben?"

"No, I'm not."

"And is it the *here*, do you think?—or the *with Ben?*"

Instead of answering she began to cry, big racking sobs that shook my bed too.

"Aw," my aunt said. "Aw." This went on for what seemed like a long time. My mind began to wander, but then the crying stopped, and Audrey blew her nose. "I'm an idiot," she said, "to do this to you. And on your last day here too—I guess that's why I did it." And she gave a little sobbing laugh.

"Would you like me to go down and tell Ben where you are?—and then we could go for a walk and talk some more?"

"Yes, but . . . don't you want to sleep now? I'll be all right."

"I know you will, but let's walk, we haven't walked in the morning, I'm always asleep, and I don't want to sleep this morning. I'm going to ask Ben for some coffee, to bring back up. I'll bring a cup for you—shall I? Would you like to stay and wait for me here?" I heard her bare feet on the floor, then her shoes. Audrey was silent, only sniffling once or twice. Dim and expectant, I lay dozing, and fell asleep. When I opened my eyes my aunt was sitting on my bed.

"Sleepyhead."

I sat up.

"Look," she said. I looked out. The sun was bright now on the wet grass. An unbroken, gradually broadening funnel of smoke floated up from the kitchen chimney and faded away in the sky. "So this is morning," my aunt said. "It's almost as beautiful as being asleep."

"Audrey woke you up," I said.

"Sure did." She raised her hand to remind me, Audrey was there, on the other side of the partition, sitting on the bed probably, waiting. "And Ben is sad," my aunt said. "But he's making pancakes, mostly for you, I think, and he sent you a message." She made her voice deep: " 'Tell him they'll be ready when he is.' Well, this is our last day."

I nodded.

"But only till summer, for you."

IV

Monday, May 5

Dear Myron,

A sad thing, Kate's passing. I'm sorry to hear it for my sake too. Please thank Anna for letting me know.

Audrey left. I wish I could say I think she'll be back. I'm hobbling around here on crutches myself—so here's to better times coming!

If Maxie's still able to come this summer and wants to, I'll be here. Plans haven't changed in that regard.

Your friend,
Ben

Monday, May 19

Son,

That's good. I'll be glad of the help and the company.

Yes, I'm wearing a cast—big heavy one, but just from the knee down. For how long? I asked that too, but the man won't say—as long as it takes, he says.

We were up on top of the last wagonful of meadow hay—another fellow and I—coming in along the sidehill, almost

to the barn when I spilt the load—turned the wagon clear
over upside down. But it flung us out a ways down the hill—
we might have been bad off otherwise. Well, it won't be
long now.

   Best to your dad and that good-looking aunt of yours,
                Your old partner,
                    Ben

My aunt arranged it so that I could come to her office every day
after school. After I got there she would take me across the street
to the coffeeshop, where she knew everybody. Afterwards, back
in her office, while she talked to clients I'd listen through the
closed or almost-closed door, not to hear what was said but just to
pick her voice out from the others. On my side it was a love affair
in which there was very little risk and very little pain—as long as
she didn't disappear off the face of the earth as my mother had—
which is what I always feared. On her way home she'd let me off
in front of the old three-story building where my father's lab
was—not seeing him herself.

One night my father looked at me and said to Rose: "Anna is
here so rarely now. You and I hardly see her."

"Don't invite her if you don't want her to come," Rose said.

"But I do want her to," he said.

"Well—?" Rose said, and turned away.

The next night my aunt came to supper. He had asked her—
as simple as that! it seemed at first.

We sat down, just us three. Maybe my aunt wanted to say, or
wanted him to say, something about my mother, but no one did.
My father was happy and cheerful until he noticed—which he
never even would have done before—that my aunt looked unhappy. Then he reached over and patted her on the head as if she

were a child or a cat—which made her look more unhappy still. At that moment she told us she was going to go on a trip, and when we asked her why and when and to where and for how long, she said she didn't know yet, she wasn't sure.

The night before she left, I saw him sitting in his study. I'd been with her as usual that day, and as usual he hadn't. He was at his desk, with the phone pressed to his ear, his head tilted to the side. One of the yellow pads he usually doodled on was in front of him and he had the usual pencil in his hand—but his hand wasn't moving. Whatever was coming through the receiver had his attention.

I came back when he was done. "Why is she going?" I said.

"Well," he said, shrugging, "to be by herself, she says, to look out the train window and think."

The next morning while I was at school he took her to the station.

In the days following, my father and I still came home together from his lab. He'd watch me run to the mailbox. After the third day cards began to come, but only for me.

On the first one was a photograph of the side of a mountain, a train trestle and a train. I turned it over:

Dear Max,
I brought a book but so far I'm too lazy to read it. I like seeing backyards—better than mountains. At night we go through people's sleep—and change their dreams, I think.
    Are you glad you can't write me?
    The train sways—and jiggles too—as I see when I try to write—or eat—which is what I do mostly.
                                          Love,
                                          Anna

On the second card was a photograph of a girl, lying on her belly, crosswise over the back of a horse. The horse had turned its head to look at her, so their faces were close together. The girl was pretty, looked only thirteen or fourteen, and had long hair.

Dear Max,
Does she remind you of Audrey? She does me—except that she wants to kiss the horse.
Hundreds of miles of wheatfields—I look away and look back and see the same thing—which only shows I'm not very observant of differences. I'm becoming giddy, from wheatfields, or from being so much alone, but it's good for me, I've decided, for now. Soon you'll be leaving too. Don't forget me.

Love,
Anna

The cards came, this went on, but nothing came for my father. "Is it to you?" he'd ask, bashfully. "May I see?" And I'd hand it to him, and watch his face.

Until one day I pulled a letter out of the box: the familiar neat small writing. Through the envelope I could feel the folded sheets. When I pressed them down they sprang up again. What could she say in so many words?

"For you?"

I shook my head.

"Ah," he said, and took the letter off.

We came around a curve and saw the river. "Now we really are almost there," I said.

"We really are," my father said.

The car rolled slowly over the metal roadway of the bridge. I
put my head out the window. I could see the guidepoles sticking
up out of the water down below. "There's the ford," I said.
"Where the trucks cross. Look!" The steady current pushed a
constant ripple over the edge of the cement. I could see the slab
itself, almost. My father patiently looked. "See?"

"I see," he said.

A minute later, past the bridge and out of sight of the river,
"It's two o'clock," I said, looking at the car clock, which my father could also see. "Ben won't be in the house. . . I wonder how
he works on crutches?"

"We'll soon see," my father said.

"I wonder if Audrey took the donkey?"

"I don't know," he said. "We'll soon find out."

Around another curve, we came to the town. "Jacksonville,
population 200," I said, reading from the sign that was in plain
sight. Four old men sitting outside the post office–store turned
their heads.

A little farther, the moments and curves growing longer—
then we saw the barn, the house and the hill above them. "Can
we park where we did last time?"

"We may," he said. We bounced across the ruts.

"There!" I said. "No! There! Don't you remember?"

The hill that had been green was brown. The sky, the barns,
the house, the orchard (a deep green now, blossomless, dotted
with apples)—in the jump from spring to summer everything
was different, changed beyond recognition, I felt, and for a moment my heart sank. At the spot where the path came down from
the spring, Ben failed to step out and greet us. I climbed the corral fence, pressed my hands down on the edge of the rough top
board. A lower board pressed up hard through my boots against
my feet; I began to feel again the sameness of things.

I looked for the donkey: Inside the barn were baby twin calves, with new faces so white they gleamed in the dark. No donkey, but even if Audrey had taken him with her, that didn't mean she might not decide some day to come back. And even if she didn't ever, that didn't mean Ben couldn't hope that she would—as long as they both were alive.

We walked toward the house. My father was cheerful. "If Kate were to sit in the orchard now," he said, stopping, "so many apples have fallen—and are still falling—look at them all on the ground . . . But I suppose an apple falling from so low a height is hardly dangerous—they're rather small, I suppose from there being so many . . . but sweet. Taste!" He handed me an apple.

We stood by the back door. "You knock," I said.

He smiled at me, shrugged, walked up the wooden steps and knocked on the screen door while I hung back.

On the way up in the car, when we would stop he would write down things that he had thought of—parts of sentences with mathematical symbols in them. But even while he was driving, when he must have been thinking of the things to later write down—even then he wasn't as abstracted as he used to be. All these last days he was happy and could work and think. "I miss Kate," he said, "but whether I miss her illness too, I find hard to say."

No one came to the door. I went up the steps and pressed my nose against the screen—and saw the crown of one of Ben's old felt hats up high against the wall, probably hanging on a nail.

It was dry and hot; in the sun it was very hot. We stood in the shade of the oak. When you stood still you could feel the air move. I pulled a bunch of small dusty-looking green grapes from the big vine that Ben said was almost as old as the oak. The grapes were warm to the touch but cool in your mouth and sweet and satisfied your thirst. I picked some for my father.

"Thanks," he said. "All our lives, your mother has liked, did like, to sit out . . . oh, in the shade, in the sun, under a tree, on a bench, in the grass—it mattered very little where—to sit out-side and read—to read almost anything. Time concentrates it-self into so few images—the mind is a rather odd apparatus really."

"We should find Ben," I said.

"Where shall we look?" he said.

"Everywhere."

"Everywhere at once? Where should we start?" he said, still fondly, still cheerful. "Ben is a generous man."

"Why?" I said.

"I've no idea."

"Why do you say it?"

"Oh . . . I remember—various things—surprisingly enough. Even people who remember badly remember. Well, I'll follow you."

As we started around the corner of the house a woman, wear-ing a hat but no shirt, holding a trowel, eyes soft with surprise and fear, stood up in front of us. Pink already from working in the sun, streaks of a darker color appeared like magic on her throat, crossed her collarbone and spread down to her breasts, which she covered as she turned away not saying anything and picked her shirt up from the rail of the gallery.

"We're very sorry," my father said, looking to the side. "It's hot—a hot day."

She pulled her shirt on over her sticky arms and shoulders and with her back to us buttoned it from the bottom up, then turned.

"What can I help you find?" she said. There was reserve some-how in the angle of the man's hat, in the loose-fitting shirt, in her voice.

"A person," my father said, smiling awkwardly. "We're looking for Ben."

"This is his place, they're on the other side of the hill, baling," she said.

"Thank you, thank you very much, we'll look there. And incidentally . . ."

She nodded when he introduced himself and again when he introduced me, after which he paused. At the last moment she took a step forward and held out her hand. "Lucille," she said.

"Do you think she's . . . she's Ben's girlfriend now?" I said.

"Well, we . . . should at least wonder if she is," he said.

The hill was sheepless now, and the sheep had eaten all the grass. Puffs of dust rose up under our feet as we climbed.

There were four haybarns, one above the other on the hill. We came to the first one. The big wooden shutters were open, for the hay to breathe. The hay was light green, had been piled in loose, and smelled like mown grass. That was meadow hay. I tried to remember what he had said in the letter: ". . . up on the last wagonload of meadow hay, another fellow and I, almost to the barn when I—" Higher up, I could see the next barn, and beyond that, because I knew it was there and looked, among the oaks the roof of the third. "—when I spilt the load," he had written. Not, when the load spilt but when I—Ben—spilt the load. We stopped in the shade of the barn.

"It's hot," I said.

"But what is it that's hot?" my father said.

"Climbing the hill," I said.

"Not you, not the hill, but climbing the hill—that's right," he said. "Or . . . we could say: 'Measured by the sensations of a self-propelled person on a warm day, uphills are hot'—then try out other hills to see if we're right."

"Not today, it's too hot," I said, and he smiled.

It dawned on me that logic was no good for figuring things out with, but it was good for checking afterward to see whether you had. "I wonder where Ben broke his leg," I said.

"We'll have to ask," my father said.

We were climbing again. The hill was steep. But up ahead, higher, it was steeper. Now, in summer, it was dry, with good footing for the horses, and good traction for the wheels. But in the spring, if it was wet . . . I tried to imagine wet rocks, wet clay ground, the horses' wet slippery shoes, the metal-rimmed wheels of the wagon, and the wagonbed itself, wet and slick. If everything was wet, then how could it have been Ben's fault? The load would slip and shift its balance, the wagon would slide sideways on the steep hill, the team jump or shy and try to bolt. But then I remembered again how in his letter he had said: "I spilt . . ."

We stopped in the shade of the second barn too, climbed again to the third, rested and climbed to the fourth. It was a long way.

The top of the hill was broad, like a fat cow's back, and flattish, so that we couldn't tell where the peak was until we'd already gone over it—and even then we couldn't see beyond the slightly downsloping ground just in front of us.

We came to a fence. My father held the wires apart for me; I climbed through, then held them apart for him. Beyond the fence, where no sheep or cattle had been, the wild oats stood high as my face. They brushed against us as we walked—the stalks slim, pale, light nearly as air, the seed clusters empty.

We heard the baler somewhere ahead below us, muffled at first and faltering, then louder but just as erratic.

I'd grown used to seeing only a little way ahead—then all obstructions vanished. Across a gap, under the sky, we saw a ridge, and at our feet a long steep slope down to a valley, flat-floored, yellow with oats (some cut, some still standing, some raked into windrows), and, with men around it, just below us, the baler, hitched to a pair of round-looking, idle-standing horses. I saw a tall man with a long fork, in long motions pitching hay from a pile on the ground up into the baler's high mouth, where a big rust-colored metal arm punched it down. Was that Ben? I tried to make it be by looking, forgetting, even, his leg. At the moment of disappointment my eye was taken, at the far end of the field or valley, by a single red-colored horse, coming out from under a clump of oaks, pulling a light buckrake with a man sitting high up on the rake's seat, moving in a smooth, fast circle through the stubble and the mown oats. "There's Ben," I said. "Look!"

"It would be more surprising if it were someone else," my father said, laughing. "Let's go down."

"Look—look at his leg," I said.

"Yes, I see—it's propped out in front of him."

The men around the baler saw us moving on the hillside and stopped to look. Ben saw them looking, saw us, stopped his horse, sat a few seconds, looking, decided who we were, waved, and waved us to come on. Then he took off raking again. But when he saw us get nearly to the bottom of the slope, he came to meet us at a trot.

The foot of the cast, wrapped in burlap sacks, rode in the cleft of a forked stick fastened to the frame of the buckrake. Ben sat up straight on the spoon-shaped metal seat.

From a little way off, all three of us called out, but to be properly greeted my father and I had to walk up one at a time in the space between the horse's tail and the rake. My father let me make him go first. Ben held the lines in one hand: the horse— Jerry, I recognized him now—stood quietly, breathing big breaths, sweating a little, shining, and flicking his ears. I could see the back of my father's head, and Ben's face (oblong and gaunt), as they talked, ". . . your great loss, sir," I heard Ben say.

I saw my father answer. Ben looked solemn and nodded. My father said something more. Ben's expression changed, and he said: "Thank you, Myron. No, I don't think there is, no chance at all, this time." His mouth pressed itself into a line, then he opened it again. "She made it clear as glass. So I've put it behind me now."

My father spoke. Ben smiled. "That's right," he said. "If it was easy as that, they wouldn't sell much whiskey, would they." Then my father motioned toward Ben's leg. Ben slapped the cast with the leather lines, not hard. "Broke it the day she left," he said. "Gave me something else to think about, anyhow."

Ben asked if we'd like to go back to the house and relax. We said we'd rather work, and he said he could oblige us. "I'm behind," he said, and thanked us.

"It's a very large field," my father said. "It looks like a fine harvest."

"It does from a distance," Ben said.

He drove the horse slow, toward the baler. My father and I walked alongside the hooped tines of the rake as they flashed and bounced.

The baler made a terrific racket. When we were close enough to see the chaff swirling in the air above the machine, the men turned to look at us and Ben held his hand up in the air and flicked an imaginary switch. Someone touched a real switch then, and the noise and work and even the swirl of haydust in the air stopped.

We were introduced, and after a bit of conferring two of the four men went off to finish unloading hay from the truck; my father and I were put to work on the baler and given the easiest jobs.

The machine started up. Ben raised the reins and said he would see us in a while. Facing the half-made bales I sat on the narrow wooden bench that was bolted to the machine. My father poked the baling wires through from the other side, I found the ends and tied them together the way Elmer had shown me. But as the rake moved away I turned and watched. It was smooth in motion and wrapped in its own quiet. The horse's hips worked in silence under the harness, and Ben too moved without effort, sitting still—as if he were in motion and immobile at the same time.

Later, when I turned my head and twisted my body I could see Ben at the far end of the field circling. Once I couldn't find him and searched with my eyes till my father had to call to me through the space between the bales. I tied the wires and turned to look again. Under an oak I saw the horse's light-colored tail switching, then half-saw, half-imagined Ben, sitting on the parked rake, still as the tree itself, resting in the deep shade.

Elmer forked the hay into the mouth of the baler. John pulled the made bales out at the back end and stacked them. My father separated the half-compacted hay into bale lengths by shoving in wooden blocks at intervals, and inserted the wires too. The air was full of chaff and noise. We sweated; the dirt and hay that stuck to our skin mottled us dark. When Elmer stopped the machine we stood on its shady side and passed around the waterbag. John was taciturn, Elmer talked. As he was getting ready to start up the baler again, he scraped the side of his boot along in the dirt and said half to himself: "Oats all over the ground. It's a shame."

"Oh," my father said cheerfully. "Should they be in the hay?" He looked at Elmer's face and added, "Ah! Then it really is quite serious."

We hadn't been back to work long when I saw a car coming along the edge of the field, through the stubble. Elmer switched the baler off and tossed his fork into the haypile. "Another hay buyer, John," he said.

A man about sixty, a little portly, got out of the car. Elmer stepped toward him. "Webber?" the man said.

"That's him on the rake, down at the other end," Elmer said.

"And this is the hay?"

"Eighty acres of it," Elmer said.

The man scraped the side of his shoe across the packed dirt by the baler, like Elmer had. "Oats all over the ground," he said.

"Some," Elmer said.

Bending down, he and Elmer untwisted the wires on a bale. The man spread the packed hay apart in one place, then another, stood up again and shook his head. "Oat hay without oats. Sorry, boys."

His car bounced slowly away along the edge of the field, the way it had come. But Ben had seen him now, and came crossing the field at an angle, his horse pulling the rake at a jog, while we stood and watched.

"Was it just that the weather has been unusually dry?" my father said.

"We expected that—hasn't been unusual," Elmer said. He nodded toward Ben: "Look there, he's going to intercept him." Then he went on: "New man in the country's last in line for the baler. And we broke down, how many times, John? before we got over here with it?"

John shook his head.

The rake reached the edge of the field, politely headed off the car, and the car stopped.

"And . . . how severe a blow will it be, to Ben?" my father said.

"Well . . . it's a big field," Elmer said. "Yield maybe four hundred ton, maybe more. And good oat hay's selling for what, John?—thirty-two, thirty-four dollars a ton?" (John moved his head.) "He'll be lucky if he gets fifteen for this." (John made the same motion again.) "That's quite a shortfall."

"And Ben is . . . expecting the lower price?"

"He is now. He wasn't, but he is now. These oats won't jump back in the sockets, he knows that."

The buyer got out of his car, he walked up to the rake. We watched in little glances as he and Ben began to talk.

"And do you think—pardon me for asking—that Ben will be able to handle the loss, sufficiently well?"

Elmer had been looking at Ben. He turned to my father. "No," he said.

"Thank you for telling me that," my father said.

"It's the only cash crop he had, outside a few sheep," Elmer said. "It's a hard-luck year, for him, hard enough for two years. I was with him on the wagon, when he ran off the track. He hadn't had much sleep. He'd come back from town the day before and found his wife gone. It was a flyer. But he'll just clamp his jaw and go on now, won't he—same as you or I would. Go back maybe and do what he used to do, for a while. Save up some more money."

The cast caught the sun. Ben's hat dipped down to cover his face: he had stopped talking. The buyer rested his forearm on the rump of the horse, taking his ease. Then he and Ben shook hands.

When the buyer had gone Ben drove the rake over to the baler. My father, ashamed for the moment of being rich, gave Ben an encouraging smile, and no one said anything but Elmer. "Sell it?" he said.

"Sold it," Ben said.

"That's best," Elmer said. "Sell it and go on."

In the evening, after the work was done, we all came back to the house. Lucille wasn't there. Ben said that while the rest of us went to the river to bathe, he would wash himself and then start something cooking. In answer to that, my father had only begun to say that he would rather stay at the house with Ben than go to the river, when Ben, thinking my father was only being kind, raised his crutch. "Are you and I going to have to have it out, Myron?" he said. And my father laughed and gave way.

So we drove down to the river. Elmer went first into the water, carrying the bar of soap; we followed single file, feeling our way along the immersed slab of the underwater road, six of us altogether, dirty, work-weary, naked and tenderfooted.

Ahead of me, among the hard white bodies of the others, my father looked pink and unused, as if he would last longer.

Elmer stopped at the sixth or seventh pole in, leaving one for each of us to hold onto, and with a whoop of pleasure dropped into the current. Afraid of all new things, at first I had been afraid. But it wasn't dangerous, the river wasn't deep, or very cold. The current carried you out to the length of your arms, made your arms feel long and your body long-drawn out. Elmer soaped his face and hair, ducked under, bobbed up, shook the hair out of his eyes and laughed.

I closed my eyes and put my head under too, came up, then simply hung there. Elmer would pass the soap to John, John would pass it to my father, who would pass it to . . . It would come to me—but that was not now: it was good to have time; knowing you had time, that kind of time, was bliss. I thought of Ben. In his mind's eye he would see us in the river. But he would not want us not to have pleasure just because he couldn't. He might not be happy, but still he would be pleased. My father used to be pleased too, when people did things he couldn't do, when my mother was alive. My father was still pleased with other people's luck, but it was easier to be that way now, because he was lucky himself now—and Ben was unlucky. So Ben was the way my father used to be . . . which meant that they were alike. It would be easy to list the ways that my father and Ben were different. It was harder to find the ways that they were alike. But if you could do that, it was good, because then you could learn to be like them both, at once. That was a new thought, and came to me in a new way—as if the river, not loud but never stopping, had the power to fill my mind from the outside, and connect everything.

V

Ray, Eddie, Herb—Ben said hello to them. Ray was the bartender. When he bent over, the back of his apron raised up like a skirt and you could see the pistol in a holster by his belt. Herb was old. He had given Ray all the money he had, which was a lot—eighteen thousand dollars—to keep for him so that he could live and drink until he died. Ray paid Herb's rent in the hotel across the street, and Herb drank, and sometimes ate a little, and talked to people in a friendly way, though he didn't always recognize them, and recited Shakespeare—whether well or badly nobody could tell. Eddie owned the bar. He was a friend of Ben's. Once they drove to Sacramento together. But to me he always seemed more remote and preoccupied than Ray or even Herb, or Rita, who had the lunch counter in a separate smaller room at the back with its own entrance. I was the only child who spent time in the bar. But in Rita's sometimes there were others, mostly boys who frightened me with their toughness, which seemed very real to me and may have been—while the toughness I tried to show to them I knew was not real at all. The grown-ups though were kind or cordial or ignored me.

Only once, I remember—later in the summer—a man about twenty-five told me to plug in the jukebox while another older

man was playing a harmonica. I was climbing down from the bar-
stool to do it when Ben said to stop. But that was a stranger with
a girl and we never saw them there again. Almost everyone who
came in, Ben knew—either from the bar itself or from somewhere else or both. But most of this I found out later. Today there
was hardly anyone there because it was only ten o'clock—and
Ben only had a cup of coffee, waiting for the mail to come in at
the post office. Then we were going "up on the mountain,"
where Lucille was. Ben said it was cool there and that I would like
it. While we were waiting he played "To Each His Own" on the
jukebox, and after it played he gave me another nickel to put in
and asked me to play it again. Neither Herb nor I minded and
probably Ray didn't either, he had heard it so very many times.

We went into the post office. It was hard work for Ben to climb
up the steps on his crutches, but I suppose he was afraid I might
look into the wrong box, or at least that he would never be sure.
He looked, and looked again. It was empty. "Don't know what I
pay rent on it for, do you?"

I shook my head.

"Ask at the window, son, would you, and make sure the mail's
come, and been put in the boxes. Ask about that: say, 'Has it
been put in the boxes yet this morning?'"

It had. We went out, and stood for a moment at the top of the
steps.

"Well, if you feel sorry enough for yourself, you'll melt, I imagine, in this weather. Don't you think so?"

"No," I said, solemnly. This amused him for some reason and
he laughed.

We drove east, not climbing much at first, two or three miles
of gentle curves, and came to Sonora, where Ben went into the
bank and deposited my father's check. Then he wrote a check to
Audrey and mailed it in an envelope he'd brought with him

ready, addressed to her parents' house, and without a note, because, he said, they would open it when they saw his writing.

We went on, driving east. The curves got sharper, and we were
always climbing, though not steeply. At first the trees we passed
were oaks, like on the ranch, then oaks and small pines, then
mostly pines, and then bigger pines, an occasional meadow, and
drift fences to keep the snow off the road in the winter. I was glad
to be alone traveling with Ben. I knew that his unhappiness
added somehow to my happiness, but I also knew that I didn't
want him to be unhappy.

"I said to your dad when he offered me the loan: 'I've had a run
of hard luck, maybe it's over now.' And he said to me: 'Time in its
painful aspects passes slowly.' Made me feel a little better, I don't
know why. He's a good man, your dad." Ben smiled, but then his
mood changed quickly again. "She took so little with her when
she left . . . " He passed his hand through the air between his face
and the windshield—as if there were a gnat there or a spiderweb
that he wanted to catch or brush away. But there was nothing
there. "Funny thing, a whole day'll go by now sometimes and she
won't cross my mind once. She's gone, this time—that's why I
accept it easier . . . I used to lie awake nights and watch her sleep
. . . When he set these bones the doctor said, 'If I don't put you
out, you're going to feel it.' And I said, 'Try me awake. I've got to
go back home.' I was afraid she might come back and me not be
there."

We drove along. Sometimes he would say something, his
mind full of the past. Events were running through his head—or
not events really or even memories, but pain. He only told me
snatches of it then, and even they were said mostly to himself
. . . He told me how one evening, at the end of April, he'd taken
her to the fair in Sonora, where there was a rodeo. A Roman
rider, a man, jumped a pair of horses through a flaming hoop.

"Audrey could have done that, you see. A good-looking young woman—the crowd would have liked it even better. I remember sitting there in the bleachers thinking, 'She could be doing that, right now.' And she was sitting there beside me thinking, 'That's my life, and I'm up here watching it pass by.' And we wouldn't either one of us speak about that, and that kept us from speaking about anything." Then a young woman did ride out on the track in front of the grandstand. A trick rider. She ran her pinto horse up and down in front of the people, flung herself into all kinds of extreme positions with exotic names, which the announcer called out: The Wounded Princess. The Cherokee Death Drag. They both sat silent. Why pretend she would ever trick ride now? She was living his life now. She only had to get used to it. But she looked unhappier, day after day.

One morning in early May, he got up at five, ate. She was asleep. Elmer's truck pulled in. He met Elmer at the barn, they harnessed the team, took the wagon up onto the hill, forked the cut, curing meadow grass onto the wagon from the windrows till they had a load, hauled it in to the uppermost barn and forked it through the window on top of what was already there. Then with the same forks, in the morning sun, walking carefully on the rough slanting ground, they turned over a couple more windrows, for the air and warmth to penetrate: they would bring that in too, tomorrow, when the dew was on it. They were done by ten. The plan was, in the afternoon Ben would take a dozen lambs to Modesto to sell at auction. He was going to use Elmer's truck. Elmer said he'd go along for the ride; and Audrey might too, if she liked. So far, she wouldn't say.

When they were unhitching the team Ben saw that the singletree, which he'd just bought in Jamestown the week before, was split almost through. They needed one tomorrow, to bring in that next load. He would take it back to the store where he'd bought it—if Elmer could take the lambs. He could, sure, he said.

And she said she would stay home. When he left for Jamestown she was in the kitchen. She waved to him. Elmer had the truck backed up to the loading chute. Ben had offered to help him load, but Elmer said not to bother—it was easy to load lambs, and the longer they were in the truck the more they'd shrink.

He came back that afternoon around three. The truck was gone all right, as it should be, he saw that first off. He pulled his car up by the house. His heart sank for a moment when he didn't see her either at the window or anywhere outside, but he often did not see her and his heart often sank, so he took comfort now in that. The kitchen window was shut. There were no screens, and she shut it whenever she was going out for long. He went into the house. She had gone out, but maybe she had already come back. He walked through the kitchen, along the gallery, through the front room, and glanced into the bedroom and called to her. No, she wasn't there. He came back out and walked to the barn, carrying the singletree, which he picked up out of the car. He looked through the fence and was glad to see the donkey gone. Sometimes she rode him down to the river where there was a sandy margin to lope along, sometimes up to the spring. He set the singletree down by the wagon. He walked back to the house, went back inside and into the bedroom. He stopped just inside the door and turned his head slowly. Her purse was gone from the bureau, her jacket from its hook in the closet. He felt the blood rush to his face before he could think. Then he turned and saw what he had seen out of the corner of his eye the moment he came through the door—a piece of paper on the bed.

He stood near the window, with the light behind him, and held it out at arm's length. She had printed—square well-shaped letters, like all the few notes he had got from her over the years. (Later he found other versions of it, pieces of them, all saying almost exactly the same thing, in the stove—though she could not have had much time.)

Dear Ben,
The rodeo stock contractor in Modesto will either give me work or tell me where to look. Don't blame Elmer. He doesn't want to take me.

But then the last part she had written quickly in small script, crooked letters:

I'm scared and ashamed. I will be all right. I hope you will be all right too.

He walked through the rooms. At first it was like a piece of violence, something broken that his imagination could not keep from mending. He saw her gone finally forever, at one moment, coming back at the next, or even having never left. But he became calmer within minutes, folded the note and put it in his shirt pocket. He even felt reflective, like a reasonable man— he noticed it himself, was surprised and glad, glad because he wanted to survive and be well.

He walked out toward the barn again, thinking. She had taken so little: the smallest suitcase, like a child. He stepped— bending low—through the sunken side door of the barn. In the tackroom one dusty ray of light slanted in through the window. He stood waiting till he could see. A halter, the donkey's bridle, those were gone from the pegs. Another peg was bare— what . . . ? Sure, a lariat. From the saddle racks, the little surcingle she used sometimes was gone, and a saddle blanket. He felt inside the box where they kept the brushes and currycombs. She'd taken one brush. He held the other one up in the light; but even when he saw it, he couldn't tell which one it was. It was strange how curious he was. He ran the back of his hand over the bristles (as she had done too maybe; this was the soft brush and she would want the stiffer one, the hair of the donkey's coat was long and rough). He imagined her hand passing over the smooth wood, passing over the bristles, but he was still calm. She loved to be in motion, her own motion, the donkey's motion—but she did not like the horse's motion—Jerry's—very much. Why was that? He put his hand in his shirt pocket, pulled out the note and unfolded it, held it out in the light. She didn't like words, she had left without many. He had always known she would. There was cowardice in that way of leaving, and bravery too. He caught himself summing her up and stopped. Careful to duck, he went back out. Even in the shade the day was bright. He stood blinking. What to do?—too much time—how would he pass it all if she—? But was it impossible—she—would she never—? Then it was as if his mind reversed itself. The truck would pull in and . . . on the passenger side behind the windshield he saw a faint dim presence. The truck door opened; high up, she, small, not faint now, solid and agile, climbed down carefully, and when both her feet were on the ground she raised her head and looked him full in the face, as she had not done for a long time: a lovely vision, a comfort, yet so unlikely that it frightened him to see it.

When Elmer drove in an hour later, Ben—standing out in the rutted driveway—was looking so hard at the windshield of the truck, with the sun behind it, that Elmer was scared for a second: the man might do him harm. But no, that was wrong, he saw which half of the windshield Ben was looking at. Elmer got out, Ben still staring up at the empty truck, and walked up to him quickly. "I wanted no part of it," he said, and Ben said: "No, I know. Lambs get sold all right?" Elmer gave him the check, Ben looked at it, folded it and put it in his pocket. "Come on in, have some coffee," Ben said.

Elmer sat down at the table, Ben with his back to him at first, at the stove. "I took her where she asked to go. Didn't know what else to do."

"You did right," Ben said.

"I tried to get her to stay home," Elmer said.

"She's free to come and go," Ben said.

A space of silence, then Ben said: "Did you let her off at Hicks's place?"

"She didn't say whose place it was. There was bucking stock in the field—bulls and big hammerheaded horses."

Ben nodded.

"We had the burro paneled off from the sheep. I told her, 'Let's drive on in and back up to the chute, he's got one there, I can see it from here.' She said, 'No, just stop.' So we stopped out along the side of the road. That's a high gate on the truck. I wouldn't jump a horse out of it, and a horse wouldn't jump out of it, but that burro hopped out like a rabbit when she asked him to."

Ben nodded.

"She had her little bit of tack in a towsack. She tied the top of the sack to the suitcase handle and threw the works over the burro's back, and that's how they went, up the lane, herself in the lead."

"She say anything?" Ben said.

"She said goodbye and thanks. And she said, 'Don't worry, he won't be mad.' And I said I wasn't worried. She said she left you a note."

"She did. Can you come back in the morning early?"

"To bring in that hay? I figured on it. Come on over to my place tonight though. We'll have a drink, eat some supper. Or just sit

around, where there's people. Nobody'll bother you. You can
mope there as easy as here."

Ben thanked him and said no.

When Elmer came back in the morning Ben had the team already harnessed. "Good morning," he said. "Good morning."
His big rawboned face was more rawboned, his blue eyes more
faded and lined with red. But that was all right, that was normal;
Elmer was glad it wasn't worse.

They went up on the hill, Ben driving the team, and forked up
the windrows they'd turned the day before, and were coming in
with the load, along the sidehill, heading again for the uppermost barn, when Ben missed the old wheel track by three, four
inches, and the uphill wheel rode high over a rock—the load
shifted and slid, and the wagon overbalanced . . .

"Where is she now?" I said.

"If I knew where, it wouldn't matter, would it? . . . So let's go
on and think about something else—or talk about it anyhow."

I nodded, and for a long while he didn't say anything at all.

We came to a meadow farther across than any of the ones we'd
passed before. It was round and had rising land all around it,
like a lake. Then there was another rising curve and another
meadow. We were as high up as this highway would go, the top of
the pass, Ben said. The road was straight and flat now. All around
us I could see the peaks of mountains, and on one of them, snow,
though not much. We came to a junction, where there was a
store, and stopped.

The sign said that to the right or south, twelve miles, was
Steelhead Meadows. That was where Lucille's packstation was.
And to the left, which I didn't pay much attention to at first, be-
cause it wasn't important to us yet, the sign said Cedarville, 120

miles, through a thick-looking forest, into which the road disappeared.

We got out of the car. It was late in the afternoon, bright and still, but not hot, if it ever had been hot here, and the air was not heavy.

"Let's go in," Ben said. "I owe some money."

"Here?"

"That's right. One night last spring I ran up a debt, more than one, maybe. Right here."

I wondered what he meant, but then I was distracted by a poster on the outside wall of the store under the awning. Hayfork Rodeo, it said, and had a picture on it of a man being bucked off a horse.

"Look," I said, but he was already looking.

He stopped and stood still and shrugged. "They rodeo all summer in these wintry little towns."

"Where's Hayfork?" I said.

He pointed. "Ninety miles of crooked road, that way. Be glad we're not going."

I looked again at the poster. "It was last weekend," I said.

He had started to go in but swung back suddenly and looked. "You're right," he said. "It's over. Don't even have to think about it, then."

The man behind the counter, not old but taciturn and grim-looking, barely nodded.

"I was in here one night. I want to pay for what I broke," Ben said.

The man looked him up and down. "You're Webber. I remember you."

"—And for what the other man broke, if he hasn't paid for it."

"It's been paid for."

"All of it?"

"No need to say who by, is there?"

"No," Ben said quietly. "Can you sell me a case of whiskey, then?"

"I know her brand," the man said.

"Do you have it?"

"I'd be in trouble if I didn't." Then he went into the back room and came back carrying the case of whiskey. He set it up on the bar counter.

Ben handed him a hundred-dollar bill, and only got two or three dollars back. The man brought out some letters too, and laid them on top of the whiskey, and a couple of rolled-up newspapers wrapped in brown paper. "You take this mail to her. Save her a trip."

Ben picked up the mail. The man came through the counter then, lifting up a hinged board, and carried the whiskey out to the car.

"I thank you," Ben said. "That rodeo in Hayfork—was it a good one?"

"Nobody said it was or it wasn't, to me. There's one in Cedarville just like it if you want to find out."

"Is that right? When is that?"

"Starts tonight."

"That's a long ways though, isn't it, to go to a rodeo," Ben said.

"It would be for me," the man said.

We were glad to drive away. "Sour old bastard," Ben said. "Spent too many years alone up here. He chose it, though. They'll say that about me one of these days if I don't watch out."

We drove toward Lucille's. Pretty soon the pavement ended, and we were on gravel. "Those newspapers in her mail," he said. "Where are they from? Can you tell without taking off the wrappers?"

"The *Modoc Eagle*," I said, "and the *Hayfork Times*."

"Tear the wrapping off that one," he said, slowing down. "Lucille won't mind."

With the wrapper torn, the newspaper unrolled by itself in my hands. In the middle of the front page was a picture of a bull rider on the ground crawling away from a bull that had kicked his hind legs so high in the air that he seemed almost to be standing on his nose. And in the lower right-hand corner . . . my eyes moved to it, drawn before I knew quite what I'd seen. "Look!"

He pulled over and stopped, twisted in the seat and held the paper out at arm's length. "It's her all right. Let's get out of the car." He got out without his crutches and, leaning against the fender, spread the paper out on the hood. It was a photograph of their two faces—Audrey's and the donkey's. She had on an old felt hat that made her look almost like a boy, and he had his muzzle poked up into the air and his upper lip rolled up to show his gums and teeth in a crazy kind of horse-laugh grin.

"It says something under it," Ben said.

" 'Her Hero.' "

"And is there an article?"

" 'See page three.' "

He turned the page. "Can you read it to me, son?"

There was a small photograph of the man who wrote the column, old, with a chubby face. I read the heading: " 'Audience Rapt.' "

"Rapt!" Ben said. "That's good. Go on."

" 'Expecting to see simply another between-events act created only to distract us tolerably while the cowboys hurry to reload the chutes for the next *real* event, we were taken by surprise this year in Hayfork. Not only that, but those of us who had been brought up to believe that a burro is an animal too smart, too dumb, or perhaps only too fiercely independent to train—received an education of our own Saturday night, from Audrey Webber. This young woman (yes, folks, look under that hat again), bashful and modest, without a word spoken, converted a noisy rodeo crowd into a rapt audience' "—"There it is," Ben said—" 'and became for many the muted highlight of the show.' " "Good," he said, "is that it?" " 'Later, surrounded though she was by admirers, most of them young, Miss Webber and her friend stood for a picture. To the comments of your columnist: "It must be difficult, but you make it appear so simple"—she replied chiefly with a smile. It's an act not to miss.' "

"Not to miss," Ben said.

We got in the car, started it up, drove slow. He looked thoughtful again, and sad. "Just think," he said. "If we hadn't found out she was there, we might have gone ourselves, by accident. Read it to me again, would you, son? the whole thing? Do you mind?"

I read it again.

We'd gone six or eight miles when we came to a meadow. This one wasn't round and level but irregular, slanted, and long. The road ran along the edge of it through the pines and big rocks. On every side now were mountains, or only really the upper parts of mountains because we were up so high ourselves. The horses and the mules grazing on the meadow were Lucille's, Ben said.

The sun sank and the mountaintops cast such a shadow over us that I was glad when Ben pointed to a column of smoke. It drifted up unbroken in the still air; the invisible sun struck it up high and made it silver. Then I saw the cabin chimney, then the cabin, then Lucille, sitting outside on a chunk of unsplit pine, fanning an open outdoor firepit with her hat. Flames licked up.

In the dim light and deep shade she looked like a blue shadow. She waved her hat at us and put it on.

Something moved behind her on the hillside. Then more

clearly, as they came out from among the trees, we could see three figures on horseback, followed by two bulky mules whose packs looked like part of them in the dusk and swayed as they walked. The whole mules swayed. They knew they were home now, and as I watched, they eased off the switchback trail, took a shortcut straight down, swaying more and more, passed up the men on horses and came at a rapid swaying walk right up almost to Lucille—where they stopped and stood. She spoke to the mules and raised her hand to the men, still working their way down the hill, but it was us she came forward to greet.

"Let's leave that one newspaper in the car," Ben said. "Maybe she might not like to see it."

She shook hands with me, and with Ben too, and clasped his shoulder as if he were an old friend or a brother—then suddenly embraced him. And he was awkward, more than she, and patted her two or three times on the back.

"Everybody at once!" she said, for the sake of something to say. "The boys have been out for three days. I'm glad to see them in before dark. I always worry—at least about my mules. Come over to the fire."

"Sure," Ben said. "One thing first: I tried to pay the damages up at the store . . . " He took out his billfold.

"Put your money in your pocket," she said. "I won't take it."

"You won't, won't you? I was afraid you wouldn't. Well, we brought something anyhow."

I started dragging the whiskey out of the car. "What's all this?" she said, and came to help. "A case of whiskey? You're crazy!"

"How am I? I owe it to you. I owe you more than that. I—"

"Shh," she said. "I'm glad to have it, thanks. Let's carry it in-side," she said to me. And we took it, not to the cabin with the smoking chimney—where there was a lantern burning now too, and where through the open door I saw someone, or maybe two people, crossing the room—but past that to a cabin without windows, a storehouse, dark; we set the whiskey just inside the door. Farther back among the trees I could see yet another cabin, a long low one, dark too, and the darkest part of it was the open door. Then I saw something white move into the doorway—a man wearing an apron. He stood there looking or facing out. "There's cook," Lucille said, and waved to him, but he didn't move. We started on another path through the trees. I was only sure we were going back when I saw the fire, still far away through the trees. Before we reached it, we passed a tiny clapboard shack mounted on an axle with wheels and rubber tires so you could pull it from place to place in the woods—like a sheepherder's cabin.

"That's where cook sleeps in the summer," Lucille said. "It's even worse on the inside. I hope you like it here."

Lucille was a tough, powerful woman, famous in these woods for her skill as a packer, for her ability to make a living, for the rifle over her bed, for the whiskey she could drink without being affected by it. (People said that toward the end of a long night of drinking a tiny burr would finally come into her speech—but that was the only sign.) She had a man-friend: fairly rich, a cattle buyer, mostly idle, "the bull of the woods," people called him, because he was pompous—or I heard Ben call him that. She would disappear with him for a few days or a week at a time. Rumor had it that in San Francisco or Reno she wore a dress. And the cattle buyer wanted to marry her, or liked to say so anyhow and even to propose, in public. But she said no, or more often not even that. With him she was the way she wanted to be, never passing beyond a customary good-humored reserve. But with Ben, whom she'd only taken pity on one night and meant to befriend . . . it was different. How different it was, she was still finding out. Ben had sat down outside by the fire. She sat down close to him.

He'd set his plaster heel up on a small log, to keep it out of the dirt, and was looking into the fire as if he had forgotten us all. But he looked around and smiled. Her shoulder touched his, and feelings that she knew he did not want her to have—and that she didn't want to have—passed over her face in waves.

Two men came out of the trees, toward the fire, looked at us and hesitated.

"About done, boys? Good. Come up to the fire. We've got something here to wet your whistles with."

"I'm not bashful." The man who'd spoken, the older one—about fifty, hard-looking—came up close. The younger man, about twenty, blond and bareheaded, hung back, and when he was introduced swung his head down in a strange way, almost bowing, he was so shy. Then he sat down on a piece of blanket that he had carried to the fire with him, but he sat a little ways back, as if he would like to hide his head truly—yet he had a pleasant open-featured face.

"Cool night and a fire. I've been looking forward to it," Ben said, in a friendly way.

"Warm down below?" the older man said.

"Too warm."

Lucille uncapped a bottle. The older man, who had looked two or three times at Ben, said: "I remember where I saw you."

"Where was that?" Ben said.

"Down at the junction here, one Saturday night."

"I heard I was there," Ben said.

"There was one other old boy knew for a fact you were there." He turned and said something to the shy man—I heard the word "crutch"—who nodded and glanced quickly at Ben.

"I was drunk," Ben said.

"He wished you were drunker, time it was over."

"All right, Don, have a drink," Lucille said.

"Sure it's all right! It was all right, then, with me. I enjoyed it."

"Here. See if you can anesthetize your tongue. You talk too much."

"I'll make a stab at it. Much obliged for the whiskey," he said to Ben.

"Sure thing."

Don raised the bottle in a kind of salute and took a drink. "Ben—" he said, got half to his feet and handed Ben the bottle. Ben thanked him and without drinking passed it to Lucille, who was sitting close beside him. She drank and passed it on to me. I took a sip of the burning strong stuff for the second or third time in my life, suffered, and passed it on to the shy man, who drank and passed it on to Don, who drank and passed it back to Ben, getting up to do it. "Just a short snort, Ben?" he said. "It's good for what ails you."

"Another night, thanks."

"You sure? It'll make you forget you ever were cheerful."

"What if I'm cheerful now?"

"It'll cure that too. It's a proven fact."

Ben laughed, but passed the bottle on without drinking.

A boy a little older than me came up on the shy man's side of the fire and sat down near him. He wore a hat pulled down so low on his head that the underside of the brim pressed down the tips of his ears.

"How are the mules? Happy?" Lucille said.

"They should be, they're eating," he said.

"Listen," she said.

We listened. I heard first the noise of the fire, a few crickets, a chorus of frogs far off, a bell on the meadow, and then, less loud but steady, the jaws of the mules, grinding.

"You're right," she said.

"Of course I am," the boy said.

When the bottle came he took a drink, unblinking.

"Johnny, when you get up to take the nosebags off, would you tell Michael please that we're all here, that there are six of us now—and to stir the pot."

"*You* tell him to stir the pot," he said, and she and the shy man laughed. In a little while when Johnny got up, he looked at me— which he had seemed to avoid doing before—and with careful neutrality said, "Want to come?"

The cook—he was about sixty—lived here even when every-one else was gone and the roads were covered with snow, which was probably when he liked it best. He looked up fiercely when Johnny and I came to the cabin door. "Lucille said to say . . ." —when he had heard what Lucille had said to say, he just grunted.

We waited for the mules to finish the last of their grain. Johnny asked me if Ben was my father, and then, how had he broken his leg? I told him, standing in the cold dark under the trees, using more words than I had said all in a row to anyone in weeks.

Like Johnny, I slid the nosebag forward over the mule's long thick ears, hung it up on the stub of a branch, untied the halter rope from the picketline, and, leading my mule, followed the mule Johnny was leading. I didn't want to stumble into the hind-quarters of his mule in the dark, but I was afraid of hanging back too. So I sped up out of fear one moment and slowed down the next, and my mule, impatient to go to the meadow, nudged me from behind, his nose sudden against my ribs. We got to the edge of camp, though, and Johnny stopped. I came around by his side. We unbuckled the halters, and the mules slipped quickly away from us, disappearing out from under our hands. We could hear them then, brushing against the pine branches as they moved unbothered through the dark toward the sound of the bell mare on the meadow.

Johnny went to the bunkhouse, and I went back to the fire. Only Ben and Lucille were there. When I came up I heard her say: "I know. I saw it in the paper. I wasn't going to tell you. Are you going to go?"

"Why should I?"

"I didn't ask that," she said.

"There's no hope," he said. "What would I go there for? To look at her face?"

He said it bitterly, and she answered quietly, "Probably." And to me, she said, "Come on, it's all right, sit down, supper will be ready soon, sit here and keep warm."

In what felt like some deep corner of the night someone's hand was on my shoulder. I sat up. Ben's voice was harsh and impatient, his mind and all his attention on leaving—quickly, as if it were painful to stay. And she half-helped, half-pushed him into the car, roughly, as if really she were trying to keep herself from holding him back at the same time that she was telling him to leave and was angry at him for leaving. She shoved the crutches through the open window into the backseat, and when he was in, closed the door hard. "It's too bad you can't drive," she said to me, without saying anything else. Before he could press the starter she took his face between her hands, turned his head hard and kissed him hard on the mouth, and when he began to say something said "go"—and turned and walked away back to the cabin.

He drove too fast at first, the gravel squirting and his hands tight on the wheel, but after we came to the junction (the store was only a shadow among other shadows now) and got onto the Cedarville road, he wasn't in such a hurry anymore.

"What time is it?" I said.

"After midnight awhile. Are you sleepy?"

"Not so much now," I said. "Are you?"

He shook his head.

"Will we get to Cedarville tonight?"

"Not if we don't find somebody to sell us some gas. Stations will all be closed. Lucille had some there . . . but to fill a man's car with gas so he can go look at another woman's face—I didn't have the nerve to ask. Would you?" Then after a minute he added: "Goddamn her to hell anyway, she did everything else for me—she might as well have remembered to go on and do that too. Wouldn't you say?"

But I wouldn't say.

VI

We met headlights only a few times. I got sleepy again and dozed.

Ben said: "Here's Madeline."

I opened my eyes and looked for a person, but Madeline was a town, tiny, with two gas stations this time, across the street from each other, both dark.

"We still have a quarter tank," he said. "It'll take us to Likely." I was almost asleep again when he said: "It's good not to want too much, wouldn't you say?"

"Uh-huh."

"I would too. It took me a long time to learn it. If you don't want too much, you might get what you want. If a tree don't jump out on the road first, like your dad says. They're starting to look like some of them might."

"Are you pretty sleepy?" I said.

"Just my eyes . . . So we'll pay our dollar, watch the show, and that's all. You won't mind that?"

"No," I said.

"I'll enjoy it, too," he said. "I mean, if she wasn't there, I'd enjoy just watching a rodeo anyhow. Wouldn't you?"

"Sure."

I drifted off to sleep.

"Oop!" I heard him say. My eyes opened to see a deer, big, with bright glazed eyes, just in front of us. Ben's hand hit the light button. The road went black. We went through without a crash. He pulled the lights back on, and nothing was there.

"Doe," he said.

"Where is it?" I said.

"Took off, soon as we got the lights out of her eyes. Scare you?"

"Sort of," I said.

"Wake you up?"

"Sure did," I said.

"Me, too."

We came to a flat straight stretch where the sky looked bigger. It must have been another meadow. And we passed some farm or ranch buildings, all dark.

Then we saw a light, two lights together, not a moving car, and as we got closer, not even a parked car. It was bright, though. We blinked our eyes. Two square panes of glass glowing in a metal building. We parked and got out. The building was so brightly lit inside that even the door had a sort of halo where light leaked out around the frame. Blacksmith Shop / Farm Machinery Repair, said the sign, and below that a little sign: Closed. "Won't hurt very bad to ask," Ben said.

He knocked, but there was a steady hissing noise from inside, and no answer. Ben opened the door. The bright arc of a welding torch hurt my eyes. "Don't look at it, son," Ben said, and he went in first. The man, who was big with a big neck and big arms— strong and young—didn't hear us till Ben called out. Then he turned slowly, shut off the torch and lifted his mask.

" 'Morning!" Ben said.

"I'm not open. That's why the sign says closed."

"Sorry to bother you," Ben said. "Do you know where we might buy some gas? We're almost out. We'd pay well for it."

"Nope." He struck up his torch so that the hissing noise started again, the flame leaped out, and he pulled down his mask and turned his back.

After we were well outside and the door was closed I said, "Shit."

Ben smiled. "Make you mad?" he said.

"A little," I said.

"That's right—he's too big to get *very* mad at." So we got in the car and started up again. "We'll go on," he said. "And when we come to Likely, we'll find a gas station and wait till it opens. You can stretch out in the backseat, won't be bad. It's a heck of a way to spend the night, though, isn't it?"

"I don't mind," I said.

"I don't either, right now," he said. "Hard part will be when it's over . . . unless I have a change of heart. Maybe I'll look at her and say, well, I didn't need to come all this way for that. Think that'll happen?"

"No."

"You're a pessimist."

Likely / Population 200. At the intersection there was a single streetlamp, and on one of the corners, a gas station, closed. This time we pulled in. Ben turned off the engine; but then, across the street, kitty-corner, unlit, but visible in the dim light of the streetlamp, we saw a two-story white building, and above the awning, a sign: Hotel. Ben started up the car again.

There was a light on inside. No sign said open or closed. The knob turned, and a small bell clinked once as the door pushed open. We went in, passed through the hall into the lobby, and a man's wide-awake face, round and suspicious, rose up behind the counter. "Have a room?" Ben said.

"For what night?"

"Last night."

The clock behind the desk said three. I yawned.

The man gave us the key.

Ben went up the stairs, stopping on each step to position his crutches and swing forward. Behind him, I scrooched up my shoulders and stopped and moved whenever he did—a sort of half-unconscious mimickry that I knew was out of place and was ashamed of.

The room, with its two beds, a table, a bureau and a couple of chairs, was square and clean. I put the satchels down and walked to the window. I could see the streetlamp, our car and one or two others, a few unlighted buildings, the two empty streets inter-secting, the gas station. "I think we have the whole hotel to our-selves," Ben said. He might as well have been talking about the world.

The bathroom was down the hall. He sent me first. When I came back, he had taken off his hat and his boot and was stand-ing by the bureau. When he went out, I looked at his things. He had emptied his pockets, like my father did too at night. His bill-fold was there on the bureau, a few coins, the car key, a book of matches, a sheaf of cigarette papers, the little gray muslin sack of tobacco with its yellow drawstring and the red bull printed on its side, his pocketknife . . . and, taking up most of the space, the two pages from the newspaper. Sometime while I had been asleep at Lucille's he must have gone and got the newspaper out of the car—or she had, and afterwards he had taken it apart and folded the two pages up small—I could see the many creases—and put them in his shirt pocket. And while I had been out of the room now, he had flattened the pages out again, even though he couldn't see to make out the words.

I took my clothes off and got into bed. When he came back, he sat down on the edge of a chair, sighed or groaned—more or less

with pleasure, for he was tired too—and went on undressing. He
had to work his split pants leg down off over the cast slowly.

"Good night, son. I'll have the light off in a minute or two."

"It doesn't bother me," I said.

"Long day, short pay," he said. "But we can sleep in in the
morning."

"Good night," I said.

"Good night."

I turned over toward the wall and closed my eyes, but didn't
sleep at first. I felt and heard the light go off, opened my eyes, and
heard him hop from one part of the room to another. Then there
was no noise—he was standing still somewhere, and I turned
over to look. Standing without his crutches, wearing only his un-
dershorts, he was at the bureau, smoothing out the paper with his
hands. In the dim light of the streetlamp he was almost luminous, his legs and body were as white as his cast. But his hands
and wrists and neck were so dark and thick, against the white
thinness of the rest of him—it was as if they were attached to the
wrong person. The spirit of ridicule—rooted in love or in an at-
tempt to escape from love—rose up in me again, and again I felt
ashamed.

Before dawn Ben's voice saying garbled words woke me. His face
was white and had risen up from the pillow, the cords in his neck
bulged, his eyes were open. But before I had time to even know I
was afraid, he sighed a normal long sigh, deep as a groan, closed
his eyes and sank back down. My flesh kept tingling after my
mind was calm, and I lay awake a little while listening to him
breathe—hard and uneven at first, a breath at a time, as if there
was still a nightmare in him trying to come back, but then, gradually, deep and slow.

It was early evening when we came down the last long hill.

"We're almost there," I wanted to say, as I would have to my father. We came around another curve. A billboard: Modoc County Fair / Carnival / Rodeo / Fairgrounds, 1 mile. I looked at his face, but even to look at it seemed an intrusion.

Then at last the little sign: Cedarville / Population 1,800 / Elevation 7,000. The road sloped down. I could see the line of storefronts, and people and cars and pickups on the street.

But he pulled over and stopped alongside the road, where there was still nothing but the roadside ditch, a barbwire fence, grass and trees. "We're two hours early," he said. He looked straight ahead with the motor running. Then he turned to me: "I know you'd like to see her—I don't blame you for that."

"But we will see her," I said.

"You'd like to talk to her."

I shook my head. I didn't understand what he wanted and kept my attention mainly on whether or not he would turn the key off. Would we sit here for two hours?—with the town in sight and the fairgrounds just beyond it?

"You see, if she saw you, she'd think she had to see me."

"But it doesn't matter to me," I said, my voice rising.

"You don't have to say that for my sake," he said.

That a struggle was going on in his mind I became dimly aware, but not knowing what he wanted me to say I said nothing.

"You have rights the same as I do," he said. His hands tightened on the wheel, the crease in his forehead got deeper. "You're right," he said suddenly. "It's not you who wants it. Are you hungry?"

I nodded.

"I am too. Let's go downtown and get something to eat. She'll be at the fairgrounds, I think."

The sidewalks were fairly crowded, for the only time in the year. He swung along on his crutches, keeping his eyes on the pavement in front of him, or on people's heels. But when he saw a woman's moccasins and blue-jeaned legs he looked up in spite of himself: it wasn't her. When we found a restaurant he said, "You look in."

I put my face to the window.

"Son, can you bear with me?" he said. "Could you go on inside the door and look? You'll see everybody then."

I went inside and looked at the faces of all the people eating. There was a young woman facing away from me, and I walked past her and turned around and came back. Some people were standing by the door, too, waiting, and I looked at them, and most of them looked back. I said to myself that I'd known she wouldn't be there.

But something had happened to him while I was inside.

When I came out again, he was leaning against the wall of the building with his head down.

"She isn't there," I said.

He raised his head, his face sort of gray. "I conjured her up," he said, "out of another woman—damned dumb business."

Inside, we stood by the door, waiting for a booth. A woman waiting there with her husband took one look at Ben, said something, and the man came over and said, "You take our turn, friend, when it comes up. Nobody will mind. It wears a man out standing around on those things. I know, I've tried it."

"Yes, sir, that's right," another man waiting said.

"I'll be glad to sit down, thank you kindly," Ben said.

We sat down. He faced away from the street and the windows. "I'll be all right," he said. "She's close by, it takes a while to get used to that. You order a good meal. Wasn't a bad-looking woman, either, the one I saw, different though, didn't look anything like the one I thought I saw—funny thing. Don't you take it to heart. I wouldn't myself if I could help it. I feel better now already."

But he still looked sick.

The waitress came up. She was older, and looked cheerful. Solemn and awkward, I ordered. "And—?" she said to Ben.

"Just milk," he said. "If nobody minds me taking up the space."

"We'll all be happy but you," she said.

He looked up at her and smiled.

Later, on the way out, he stopped at the table of the people who'd given us their turn. "I feel better now, thanks," he said. "I was a little woozy."

The color had come back to his face.

We walked up the street toward the car. At the corner you could see both ways to the mountains. The sun had just gone down. The thunderclouds that were building over the mountains in the west earlier had broken up, leaving streamers of color spread out in the sky. A little sheet lightning, dim, so you weren't sure at first whether you had seen something or not, flashed so far away you couldn't hear the thunder. "It's a lovely night," Ben said. "Let's put some gas in the car before we go to the fairgrounds. We'll be ready to leave, this time."

In spite of the line of cars at the gas station, he was patient now, and calm—or maybe neither, but cheerful anyway.

"Keeping you boys busy?" he said to the older man working the pump.

"Once a year, they do."

"You're used to it then. Do you get a chance to go over to the fairgrounds and take in some of the shows yourself?"

"I do. It's my station, I make a chance."

"Did you go over to the rodeo yet, this year?"

"Only thing over there worth going to, for me."

"That's about the way I feel," Ben said. "But I've never been to this one. Is it a good one? We're going over tonight."

"Oh, not as good as it used to be. Horses used to buck harder in my day. Fewer got rode, anyhow."

"Did you used to ride them some yourself?" Ben said.

"I used to try."

"I see in the paper they've put some new acts in this year."

"May have," the man said, shrugging.

"Girl with a donkey—did you happen to see that one?"

"I believe we did. Somebody said it was a girl—couldn't tell by looking. I knew it was a donkey."

"Worth seeing, was it, though?"

"Well, not all by itself—but you'll get your dollar's worth."

We parked in the big lot, which was really just part of a grassy field. In the near dark the green grass looked lush and undamaged, even under the cars. But the irregular ground was hard for Ben to maneuver on, and we were glad to get onto the graveled lanes of the fairgrounds itself. We walked toward the arena. We could see the grandstand. On the way we passed a lane lined with horse trailers and stock trucks. Ben glanced quickly down it, saw the long low roofs of the barns—where she would probably be now—and turned away.

"Do you think she's all ready yet?" I said.

"Things that meant the most to her were hardest for her to talk about. Do you remember how she used to work up at the barn by herself with that donkey, every day morning and afternoon? What was it you asked me, son?"

"Do you think she's ready yet?"

"She's all the world to that donkey," he said. "It has to be that way."

"Why?"

"All the human world . . . She never liked me to mess with him too much. Did she you?"

"No."

"If he thought one person was as good as another . . . he'd flick an ear up, say, toward the grandstand in the middle of the act . . . 'Those are all people up there, every one with a voice and hands and a right to pet me or feed me or make me do what he says . . . I'd better listen and see what they want . . . I'll get something good if I do, and bad if I don't' . . . But you see, she's all the world to him, so he pays attention to her, just to her. If I was a donkey, I would too. What'd you ask again?"

We passed through the carnival. It seemed to us that every person in front of us was going where we were and would be there first if we didn't hurry, and so without meaning to we kept walking faster—Ben swinging along smoothly—and didn't stop at all until we found the entrance booth to the rodeo. There *were* lots of people going in. We stood in line for our tickets and went in too.

As we passed through the turnstile, we saw a boy on the other side of it selling programs. Ben bought one. "Let's look and see. She might have run off again for all we know." To mention this possibility with easy-going good humor was strange, and I looked up at him. It was as if he'd convinced himself that the bad part or the hard part was over and from now on he could simply enjoy himself. Maybe it was so.

"Here it is," I said. "'Audrey Webber—The Donkey's Friend.'"

"There's truth in that," he said. "When does she come on?"

"After the steer wrestling," I said. "Between it and the bull riding."

Cedarville was a little country town, but the grandstand was

big and new, solid and square-looking from the back, with tun-
nels that led through to the front. We came out from the one we
walked through, looked up and saw long rows of benches rising,
with people climbing the cement steps, and on the other side,
below us, brightly lit, the arena itself, with an old loud-whining
rusty watertruck driving around it in circles, sprinkling the sand.
Across the arena I saw the bucking-horse chutes, painted white,
and on top of them, like a little tower, the announcer's booth.
Ben paused, looked around, then turned, and we walked along
the broad ringside aisle toward one end of the oval. The roping
chute was there, and a wide gate, and behind the gate I saw a few
men and women on horseback, waiting. That was where she
would come in, he said. But instead of sitting down low, we
climbed to a row fifty or sixty feet up, up higher than the people
down at the gate or inside the arena ever bothered to look.

And so we sat down. But even calm and quiet as Ben was now,
whenever down below us another horse and rider came around
the fence corner and into the light to stand by the gate with the
others—then for a moment he sat perfectly still.

When the grandstand was almost full the microphone began
to crackle. The announcer—I had seen him climb into his booth
up a sort of ladder—spoke out suddenly in a voice that came from
all sides at once and went on, fast and loud, though less so when
you got used to it. "Welcome," he said, "to Cedarville and the
Twenty-ninth Annual Modoc County Fair and Five-Event
World Championship Professional Rodeo . . ." Music began to
play, a recording, plenty loud too.

When the music started, riders started coming thicker and
faster to line up at the gate, till there were so many we couldn't see
the ones at the back. Some men on foot passed out flags. All the
flagbearers were women, and they wore fringed chaps, bright-
colored hats, satin shirts that sparkled under the light. The

women jammed the flagpoles into their stirrups. The flags un-
furled and the horses jumped sideways, some of them, while others tried to stand still and got bumped or jostled. "Is she here?
Will she ride in this?" I said.

"Not if she doesn't have to," he said. "Sometimes it's in the
contract."

I was more anxious and excited now than he was.

The gate opened, the music played louder, the people on
horses began to gallop in. Up in the grandstand everyone stood;
the men took off their hats. Heads turned to follow the moving
flags. Ben nudged me, I took off my hat. In a few seconds the
whole arena seemed to have filled with horses, circling. But I
kept looking at the farthest spot I could see, out beyond the gate,
till the last rider had come past it—while Ben glanced out there
occasionally, but seemed on the whole just attentive, and interested.

That was how it was after the rodeo started, too. When a horse
bucked well and the rider made a good ride, Ben listened for the
judges' score to be announced and was pleased when it was high.
The bucking horses she used to ride, I thought of—he seemed
not to. And when a little later a calf roper roped a calf, swung
down from his horse, ran the length of the rope, threw the calf
and tied it—with no wasted motion . . . "He does that like he
knows how," Ben said, as if he'd forgotten everything else. Her
face, which he said he'd come to see and had seen so often in his
mind, had seen even on the street a little while ago, had left him
in peace, for now. It was strange, I thought. I tried to understand
it, but didn't get far. Her face asleep as he looked at it at night . . .
it was not her face I saw so clearly, but his when he had talked
about it. She had been there, then she was gone. So absolute, the
difference. I could almost imagine that. Yet the violence it had
done him even when he'd known it was coming, I could not

really imagine. There was an image in my mind of Elmer's truck carrying her away, and another of her walking away up the lane, she and the donkey, with her few things, not to come back ever, and the violence he had done himself, afterwards, when the wagon tipped—but these were . . . not painful to me to think of. And he didn't seem to be thinking at all. The things he had been so conscious of a little while ago: the old shy, strong urge moving her always toward a life of her own . . . that, and even his own fear, he had driven somehow out of his thoughts. And so he sat, not suffering, not thinking, not even knowing he was hoping.

I went down to the concession stand and came back. And that quick, his equanimity was gone. When he took the coffee his hand shook and he had to set the cup down on the bench to keep it from spilling. He hugged himself and shivered. "To get in the car and go back without even letting her know we were here and saw her—do you think that's right, son?"

"I don't know," I said.

He put his hands under his thighs, hunched his shoulders and rocked a little on the bench—it made the heel of his cast rattle against the cement and he stopped and tried to sit still. "Won't be long now," he said.

When the first steer wrestler made a fast time and people clapped, including Ben and me, I felt we were clapping now not for the man's fast time, but because time itself was passing fast. We watched them go, one at a time. They all went but one, the last man listed—after him would be her. But he wasn't there. We watched to see him ride in. The chute boss called for him, more than once. The announcer called his name over the loudspeaker. We heard the chute boss say, "All right, boys, he isn't here, turn the steer out." The steer loped out by himself, and when he saw no one chasing him he slowed to a trot, turned his head to see where he was, and jumped sideways from shadows on

the ground. People laughed, but Ben shook like a leaf. Whatever
he believed, it made him feel, I suppose, that she would not be
here either.

At the far end of the arena the back gate swung open and the
steer trotted through it. Suddenly the announcer stopped talking. The arena went dark. The microphone clicked off. The
crowd shifted and, after people finished whispering or coughing,
became quiet. The prop men, like shadows, walked to the center
of the arena, carrying things we couldn't make out, then ran back
to the arena's edge. I listened hard and heard the slow long creak
of the gate down below us. The chute boss said: "Here she is, let
her in."

A spotlight came on, moved jerkily over the ground, search-
ing, and found the donkey, walking slow with his head down and
limping. And on the other side of the donkey . . . at first you saw
only her elbow and hat, a battered old felt hat. The donkey was
wearing a wooden packsaddle. She held on to its crosspiece, for
support. The crowd, that had been quiet, was silent now. She
staggered once, and when her head turned you saw that she was
an old man, with a beard—a prospector—and strapped to the
packsaddle was a bedroll, a shovel, a pan, and a canteen with its
lid dangling loose. An old prospector, out of water, on his last
legs.

She let go the crosspiece, stumbled, sank to her knees, her
body somewhere hidden in her clothes—suspendered overalls
and heavy boots . . . The donkey went on for a few steps, flicked
back an ear, stopped, turned and walked back to her. He lowered
his head. She took hold of his neck. A hush had fallen over us
all—a sort of tensing. We leaned forward. She whispered something into one of his ears, and collapsed. As she fell to the ground
there was a rustle of cloth. The sound came as a relief: she was
real, we were all real again, watching. People shifted on the

benches. But she didn't move, she wasn't moving; we were all silent again.

The donkey stood for a moment or two, his ears moving back and forth, first one then the other, like a semaphore. Then he dropped to one knee and touched her face with the rough tickly skin of his lips. She was motionless. He lowered himself carefully down beside her, to lie still himself, his little bit of bulk giving her shelter and heat against the cold air of a desert night. The spotlight went off, the whole scene went black-dark, no one could see anything (there were a few whispers), then the beam came on suddenly again in a new place, lighting up an empty patch of ground at first, then moving steadily toward the far end of the arena. It stopped: we saw an object, we couldn't make it out, the light went past it teasingly, then came back: it was a fan, an ordinary small desk fan hanging from a pole, not moving. People breathed easily, laughed. "Wind," someone said. Then the beam moved again, back the way it had come, till it came to a tree—made of willow branches tied to a pole—and under the tree a bucket with a dipper in it—you could see the handle sticking out.

Then darkness again, and we were silent though not hushed. Then in the old place the beam found the donkey just raising his head from the ground, his sweating neck glistening, his nostrils flaring and closing: he was sniffing the air. "Smells water," Ben whispered. I nodded in the dark. The donkey, then, pushed himself partway up so he sat with his front legs straight, like a dog. He raised his nose as high as he could and sniffed the air; this time, he wrinkled his upper lip, curled it back finally so far that we could see his long narrow teeth gleaming. (A child somewhere laughed.) The donkey clambered to his feet quickly now. His tiny hooves clicked together. Up, he nudged her with his nose. She didn't move. He nudged her again, nuzzled her, she still didn't move. We waited, becoming stiller. He stood, head low, as if in thought, or mourning. We were hushed. He didn't move. The complete absence of motion was like a new silence added to the old—out of which suddenly he brayed: a shattering sound, and sad, it made me want to laugh and cry together. But I didn't, and she didn't move. He took her collar in his teeth and lifted and shook her. We could hear her clothes. He lowered his head, she dropped limp back onto her knees. Still, he wouldn't let her go, but raised her up again, stood her on her feet. We could see the muscles behind his jaw and on his neck straining. She didn't fall this time. When he let her go, we saw she was leaning against him. Her hands moved, she took hold of the crosspiece. He lowered himself, first to his knees, then all the way to his belly. She half-fell, half-climbed onto his back. Cautiously, swaying a little, like a camel, he rose to his knees, then to his feet.

For a moment, darkness—we hardly knew why. Then when the spotlight came on it was shining on the tree and the bucket. No donkey—but we knew how it would end now. We watched for him, and then we saw him as he carried her out of the dark into the circle of light. He dropped to his knees, giving still the impression of deliberate and careful slowness, even though it was happening fast now. I wanted to not breathe until it was over; instead I drew slow breaths. She sat on the sand, her back against the tree, her eyes open, her face white above the white beard. You could see the donkey's sweat because his hair shone black, but her face was only a dull white. He took the dipper handle awkwardly between his teeth, raised the dipper from the bucket, a hero. Water slopped out as he held the dipper to her lips, twisting his own head and neck in a way that looked ridiculous—and she helped with her hands.

The lights came on. She laughed, jumped up, vaulted onto the donkey's back. We let ourselves subside. It was only a show.

All around, people breathed, shifted, smiled. The donkey ran full blast twenty or thirty feet, then kicked high into the air, farted, ran twenty or thirty feet again, and kicked high again; two clowns—a girl and a donkey—that was all they were now, while people laughed and applauded. They circled the arena once, full tilt, and dashed out.

Sometime in the last few minutes Ben must have made a decision, acknowledged it to himself, then let it skip unmarked and unmentioned into the past. He turned to me, motioned for me to move closer, and whispered: "If you'd go first, she'd be forewarned."

I found my way through the lanes of the carnival to the fairgrounds at large, and when I came to the place where Ben had stopped to look down the lane that led to the barns and had turned away, I turned in, walking so fast now that I was nearly running.

In the wide dirt aisle between the first barn and the next, under a pole lamp, a group of ten or twelve people had gathered around the donkey and Audrey. I went closer. She was sitting on a bale of hay, the donkey standing beside her with a nosebag on, eating grain. I walked up behind the others and stood still. She had taken off the hat and beard. Her hair was in a single braid, pinned up to itself on top of her head. There were still streaks of white on her cheeks. One man, who had been talking to her, went away, and four other people—a family, it turned out—stepped up close to admire the donkey (whose eyes were half-closed with pleasure as he chewed) and to speak to Audrey. I said to myself that I should step forward too, right away, but I didn't—and it got more difficult.

The family was all grown-ups. The oldest woman said, almost as if she were suspicious or offended: "We've seen nothing like

that here before—I suppose other places people are used to it."
And the oldest man, her husband, said that he was an old burro-
man from way back. The younger woman was embarrassed by her
parents and said: "That was all right, miss, we liked it, that was
fine," and the younger man, her husband, said, "Yes, it was."

Audrey smiled and thanked them all and they walked slowly
away. Then two young girls, one as young as I was, stepped forward. "He's so intelligent!" the younger one, who had hung back
the most, said. "I have a *horse* that I wish was that smart. I
thought donkeys were usually—!" The older one poked her.

Audrey laughed and said: "What kind of horse do you have?"

"I have a horse too," the older one said.

"Do you ride together?"

"All the time."

"You trained him yourself, didn't you?" the younger one said.

"Of course she did! . . . He's finished eating. May we . . . ?"
The older girl put out her hands slowly toward the donkey. But
even when Audrey let them pet the donkey—and they did it ex-
pertly, rubbing him behind the ears and scratching him over the
withers—still they would only glance shyly at her. And I had to
admit I was shy too, because of what I knew I should . . . Behind
her, some twenty or thirty yards away, Ben came around the corner of the barn on his crutches.

I stepped out from behind the others. Her eyes seemed to pass
me, stop and come back. She didn't have time to say anything,
but her face said: "Is it you? It's you. Then where is—" She
turned. He was walking as quick as he could. She got to her feet,
turned away from the girls and hugged him—which according to
at least one of my daydreams should have made everything all
right forever. Then she put her hand out to me. I felt proud and
came up to them, and the girls stared just as I wanted them to.
She patted me and laughed and pulled me close. "Hi," I said.

Then she turned back to Ben as if she saw nothing else. He held her by the shoulders and looked at her face. "We saw the show," he said in a husky voice. "It was a good one." He had pushed back his hat. His face looked big and white.

"That means a lot to me," she said in a whisper.

"Everyone liked it, up where we were."

Then there was a pause, and she lowered her eyes. But he didn't lower his.

The girls, embarrassed, retreated. I moved to the side.

"I know I shouldn't have come," he said. "But . . ." He stopped, and there was no answer. She bit her lip. His adam's apple rolled, down and up.

"Could we go somewhere, for a few minutes?" she said.

He held up his hand, as if he were stopping traffic. "A few minutes, a few minutes is fine!" he said.

Audrey put the donkey in his stall. I said I would wait there.

They walked together to the car. I watched their backs.

Then I sat down on a bench and leaned against the barn wall. The top half of the stall door was open, right beside me, and I could hear the donkey's feet moving in the straw bedding, and the rustle of alfalfa against the wood of the manger, as he sorted through it with his nose and lips, looking for the sweetest leaves and tenderest stems to eat first.

It was good to sit there. I could hear people, sometimes I could see them, but mostly it was voices—people feeding and watering and blanketing and rubbing down and bandaging the legs of their horses for the night, along the long rows of stalls. A few men, a few women: "It's full!" or "I'll be right back—I'm going to take the car over and get a bale of hay out of the trailer." —As if life were simple and pleasant and everyone could accomplish the things that needed to be done. But Ben's face—the image of suf-

fering love—pale, with his hat pushed back—kept rising up in
my mind too, as a sort of mystery.

Then I heard the younger girl say, "Here's his stall." And the
older one, "Here's somebody else, too," with a laugh—and the
younger one:

"Shhh."

"Hi."

"Hi."

"Hi."

"Is Audrey around?—Or the donkey?"

"Sure. I am too," I said. That was almost all. But when they'd
gone, I felt a thrill of loss—and suffered, experimentally.

The car pulled up in front of the stall. Ben turned off the engine.
Audrey got out, wiping her eyes with a handkerchief. She closed
the car door softly. When Ben got out, he left the door on his side
standing open, as if to say, *I am flattened now, the sap has all gone
out of me*. His hands and arms, when he moved on his crutches,
even when he shifted his hat back to kiss her, seemed almost too
heavy to lift. But she pressed him tight and held him.

VII

I had seen him brood, but now he sank further into himself. When he spoke he was friendly, but he hardly spoke. After a while, as we drove along back through the night, I fell asleep. Something woke me—the corner streetlamps in the little town, and I saw the dark hotel go by. The blacksmith shop, which we must have passed later, I didn't see at all, though I could only tell I was asleep by how fast the time passed and the things I missed. When we came to the junction where the store was and where the road to Lucille's was, Ben didn't stop even at the stop sign but turned toward Jamestown and the ranch. It was past daylight: I could see his face, gray and set.

We came into town about the same time of day we'd left it, but there could be no letter for him from her today, so I took his key and went up the steps into the post office and looked in the box. There was a letter lying slantwise behind the glass. I took it out. It was to me, from my father. I opened it and read it standing on the steps.

Dear Max,
We are going to be married, Anna and I. I don't expect you

to be surprised, yet there will be a shock, I'm afraid, in the news. The date will be sometime in September, when you are here to take part in the ceremony, which will be a minuscule one.

If you would feel more comfortable or happy at home now or anytime in the next few weeks, we can very easily come and pick you up. Ask Ben's advice about this, too, please, and let us hear from you in any case.

Love,
Dad

Ben looked at the opened envelope, and at my face. "From home?" he said.

I nodded.

"Bad news?"

"Uh-uh, good," I said, tried to smile, and did—but the corners of my mouth turned down.

I had got into the car, and looked straight ahead out the windshield. Instead of starting the engine, he kept looking at me, took me into account for the first time in hours. "So it's good news?" he said. "You want to read it to me?"

I shook my head and burst into tears.

"They getting married?" he said.

"Yes."

"You read it to me, when you're able."

I read it to him. The tears, still flowing, had freed the rest of me, and while I was reading I was hardly conscious, even of being unhappy. I just wished they would dry up, and by the time I was done they had.

"Just because it's good for your dad and Anna," he said, "doesn't mean it's good to you. But your mother blessed it, that's a consideration. And she'll be your stepmother. I wouldn't mind if she were mine. Well, we can console each other for a little while, anyway."

"I'm not going to leave," I said.

"Write them tonight and say Ben said you ought to think about what you want to do for a day or so. You might want to leave, there wouldn't be anything wrong with that if you did. I know you like to hang around with me—there'll always be time."

I felt as if I were under a big warm light of sympathy, which if it stayed on much longer would melt me into tears again.

"I'll write," I said. "But I don't want to leave. Let's go."

He laughed, I suppose to see me so bossy.

As we drove, he sank back into himself, but he brought himself up out of it again when we got to the ranch and went into the house. Everything seemed lonely, outside and in, because the air was still and it was the middle of the day and we were tired. There was a note from Elmer on the kitchen table. He'd been sleeping here at night and doing the chores. "Ben—" it said. "Take the calves off the cow if you want to have milk by milking time. I drank what there was. You're out of ice. I may come by with some. I mean to stop in anyhow this evening to see if you made it back all right. —Elmer."

I read the note to Ben, and he said: "You ever watch Elmer drink milk? That's something, isn't it. He's quite an Elmer. Well, hell, son, we're here—you ever make a pot of coffee?" I shook my head. "Or a pot of beans?" "No." "Fire and water's what we need. Can you build a fire, in this old stove?"

We kept busy for a while, and in the early evening, Elmer pulled in in his truck. He had come from work, and was on his way to Shorty's, where he had a room. His dog was with him, and he'd picked up forty pounds of ice for us—in one big cube—in Jacksonville.

And after he carried that in, he went back to his truck and got a bottle of whiskey. We sat in the shade on the back steps, underneath the oak tree with its big grapevine. When Elmer would throw a grape his dog would twist its head, catch it and eat it. "How's that mountain air?" Elmer said.

"We drove through a lot of it," Ben said.

"You did? I like to sit still and breathe it," Elmer said. "How's Lucille?"

"Just fair, after she saw me," Ben said.

Elmer didn't ask any more questions about the trip. He sat with us and was a comfort to Ben; they talked about the neighbors, the fish in the river, the weather, the price of cars, about Shorty's big grown dumb boys who wanted to be farmers on their dad's land when there wasn't enough of it, about the taste of the whiskey. But when he left it was night and he seemed to take the daytime world away with him.

Sometimes I didn't know whose sadness I felt, mine or Ben's. Just now he went to bed, and I did too; there was only a wall between us—and for a while I could hear him moving on the other side of it, but when those sounds had stopped, then I was left with my own sadness. Sleepy and afraid to go to sleep, I lay down on the bed with my clothes still on and the lantern still burning, yawned and closed my eyes; but fear pressed in on me, with new thoughts, though I didn't know yet what they were, and woke myself up so that I wouldn't find out. "I'll write my father," I said out loud.

But when I had written the first word—Congratulations!—I was stuck, and also felt I was a hypocrite or a liar, though even about that I was confused or unsure . . . My father had never even let his shoulder brush hers that I had seen—probably he never had . . . When he patted her on the head that night at supper, that was touching her . . . touching her as if she were a child . . . before he knew, maybe, that he loved her . . . surely before she knew that he did. That was why she got angry then or hurt and announced that she was going away. There was no reason now for them not to touch each other anymore. They would. Maybe they were now. I imagined it—that wasn't hard, because it wasn't real in my mind and I didn't know what feelings to attach to it, and it became boring, but I thought it was where the fear was and that I had conquered the fear by thinking boldly, and I took my clothes off, shut down the lantern and crawled between the sheets feeling terribly sleepy, though as soon as my eyes closed I felt the fear again.

I opened my eyes, but they closed again of themselves. I heard my father's voice. That didn't frighten me, so I kept my eyes closed and began to drift toward sleep. I heard it again, calling my mother's name, and then without expecting to I saw my mother lying on her back in bed. He was bending over her, saying her name, and his voice, which had been so peaceful a moment ago, was loud and strange. I opened my eyes, looked straight up at the ceiling and thought: it was a memory, but from when? I closed my eyes, and suddenly remembered my mother's living body with its eyes open, my father bending over and shouting "Kate!" But why? why was he afraid? I opened my eyes and sat up. I remembered. She had had a seizure and couldn't talk or move; just for a little while she couldn't; but he hadn't understood at first what it was, and he was frightened, and his fear had frightened me, when I had heard his voice, then, just as now. But why be frightened by it now? Through the open window I heard the oak tree rustle its leaves: a breeze had come up. Somewhere far off—maybe over at Shorty's place where Elmer and his dog were—I heard a dog bark. The tree rustled its leaves, stopped, then rustled them: when you sat on the back steps too you could feel how the breeze came at intervals around the corner of the house, and on the front porch you could feel it, when you sat there in the afternoons—those were the things to think about to keep from thinking. I heard Ben shift in his bed, the old rusty springs twisting against each other. It was better to both be in one room, when people felt bad; if you felt good, maybe it didn't matter . . . I didn't want to remember my mother's mouth. There was no reason to and I tried not to. Paralysis made it crooked. But the mouth of her body when she was dead was still crooked. Why was that? When she took her pills it was less the way she moved her fingers than the way she tucked the pills one at a time into the corner of her mouth and swallowed them all together that I didn't like. But if I hated to see it, why did I watch? I got up and lit the lantern. I sat at the table again and wrote, with my father's letter there too where I could see it.

> Dear Dad,
> I got your letter. I'm not surprised. Thanks for writing. I'm fine. Don't come sooner. I'm not homesick. We went to Cedarville (a town up here) and saw Audrey perform with the donkey in a rodeo. We're back now. It's pretty late but I'm not sleepy, though I am sort of. Pick me up after Labor Day as planned, but I will write again before then when I have more to say and it's not so late. And . . . Congratulations!!

I read it over and added, at the top after "Dear Dad," on the same line: "Congratulations to you and Anna!"

Before I put out the lantern I laid the letters down under the head of the bed, where I could reach out and touch them anytime I wanted to during the night.

Falling asleep, I saw a meadow like a lake, a column of smoke, the high peak of a mountain—each by itself—and my mother's face, too, alive and crooked-lipped.

Now that the hay was in, most of the work that there was to do could be put off, and we put it off—with his leg and his low spirits for an excuse. Every day he'd give a different reason why we had to go into Jamestown. When we got there, after we went to the post office we went to the bar, where Ben would have maybe two or three drinks. They didn't cheer him up, but maybe he didn't want to be cheered up. He was gloomy, and it felt good to me to be gloomy too.

I'd sit on a bar stool, listen to the talk, and if my body got restless I'd climb down and go into Rita's, where she'd let me take a broom and sweep the cafe floor.

Some mornings, Elmer met us in town, and almost every evening before dark he'd stop by the ranch, and he and Ben would talk and sometimes drink. Only the long hot afternoons were dull. Ben lay down in his room then and tried to sleep—he slept badly at night; and I'd try to sleep too, outside in the shade, but often I wasn't sleepy enough, and the flies bothered me.

Several times in July and August—early August—Ben cooked Sunday dinners. He invited Shorty and his wife and Elmer and sometimes Shorty's sons and their wives. We would all be clean and wear clean clothes and eat sitting at the table in the front room. When Ben and I did that, we pretended not to feel the way we felt—which oppresses your appetite. But the cold-bean-sandwich suppers that we ate on most nights—along with great quantities of milk and butter—kept on tasting good, at least to me.

Then on a Monday morning in August Ben got a letter, a few

lines asking him to sell her horse. That was all—all he should have expected, and after that he didn't expect anything else.

By the end of August we were spending nearly all of every day in town.

One night when we were at home asleep, a chicken squawking woke us. I waited for her to stop. If she were being eaten, let her be eaten—then she would be quiet. But she didn't stop. I got up, and met Ben, getting up too. He lit the lantern, and we went out and found the milk cow standing on the leg of a hen. I pushed her shoulder, she stepped sideways and the squawking stopped. Ben cursed and laughed in a hard, harsh way—as if not just the cow and the chicken were stupid, but everything—as if his state of mind had swallowed the world.

One evening we stopped at the Jamestown Market. We'd been in the bar (there were fourteen bars in Jamestown but we almost always went to the same one) nearly all day and were on our way home. Ben was at the counter paying. The storekeeper, to be civil, pointed to a poster on the wall. "You going to come into town Monday and help us celebrate the holiday?"

"We're in the celebrating business," Ben said. "Will the bars be open?"

"The bars will be open," the man said stiffly. "They are open every day but Sunday."

"I'll take that into account," Ben said. "Sunday's a long day, I feel that till it hurts, sometimes."

The man looked at Ben, looked at me, frowned and shook his head.

Ben pulled a long face then too, but on the way out, shuffling through the door on his crutches, he laughed so the man could hear. I felt the harshness of it, but understood only dimly what the storekeeper or even Ben might be feeling. The one thing I was still certain of, in one part of my mind, though I could see sometimes that it might appear differently to others, was that Ben must be in the right.

When Monday came, he hadn't forgotten. "It's celebrating time," he said. "Let's go in and celebrate." We were in town by ten o'clock. The Forty-nine Club was open. Old Herb was at the bar, but no one else. Ray was behind it. He had just opened up, and was glad to see us. Herb was too, though it was always hard to tell whether he remembered who you were from day to day. Pretty soon Elmer came in, looking for Ben, and sat down at the bar.

Ben handed me a quarter. Without asking what he wanted, I pushed the buttons for "I'm Walking the Floor Over You" and "To Each His Own" for Ben, and Elmer told me what two songs to play for him, and I played two for myself.

Ben and Elmer ordered whiskey and water. Ray gave me coffee free.

When "To Each His Own" came on Ben started to look morose. After all the songs had played, he gave me a nickel and asked me to play that one again. They had had another drink by then, and then they had another.

Three men came in, strangers, young workingmen wearing caps and clean overalls, cheerful looking, out for the holiday. Ben had been quiet for a while, brooding. He wanted to be like Herb seemed, immune to nearly everything, but it didn't work, or at least wasn't working. He started looking at the men. I was next to him, between him and them; but between me and them were three or four empty stools. Ben would look away from the men, then turn suddenly, as if he thought they were staring at him or talking about him. But I saw that they were paying no at-

tention at all to him, really, until he started looking at them—
then they looked at him once or twice.

When Ben turned I looked at his face. His eyes were streaked
with red; the blue parts were pale, and glittered. Elmer must have
seen about how it was. He got up, went to the door, looked out at
the street and came back, nodding in a friendly way to the men.
"Let's go out and look around," he said to Ben.

"You go if you want to," Ben said.

"You come too, do you good."

"Leave me be, I'm all right."

"I didn't say you weren't. Do you good anyhow, to get out."

"I been out, all my life," Ben said, turned his glass around,
clamped his jaw and sat still.

"You want to come out, Maxie?" Elmer said.

I shook my head.

Elmer sat down again next to Ben. "Want another song?" he
said.

"Hell no—what for?" Ben said.

"Goddamn you to hell, then, you old bastard," Elmer said,
shaking Ben by the shoulder. "Cheer up."

"I will, I'll have a drink and cheer up," Ben said, more cheerfully. But as soon as he started on the drink he was worse. He sat
with his head down, then without anything happening he
looked up and said to me: "Sit back, son, you're in these fellows'
way. They want to look at something, I'll give 'em something to
look at." He was talking right to them, but he was hardly more
than muttering. They didn't look at him, even when I leaned
back, but Elmer did, and Ray.

"That's enough," Elmer said, putting his hand again on Ben's
shoulder. But Ben didn't pay any attention to him and kept on
mouthing words at the men: they were looking at Ben now, and

the man closest to me started to look angry. I was afraid. I looked straight ahead at a row of bottles. It was strange to know so clearly that Ben was in the wrong. It was not a fact I could hold steadily in my mind—it kept slipping out. He went on, moving his mouth. The man on the end read his lips. His friends stopped talking. Behind the bar, Ray stood still. Elmer put his hand on Ben's shoulder, and when Ben turned and reached for a crutch Elmer kicked the feet of the crutches and they fell flat on the floor.

It was a hard day for Elmer. By the time we got to the end of it he was talking to Ben as if Ben were a boy, making him drink a last cup of coffee the way you tell a child to drink up a glass of milk. Ben picked up the cup, his hand shaking, and drank. "I'm a fool," he said.

"Take you this long to figure that out? You're going to drive home in a few minutes, so drink it up."

The road wound along the river. It was evening now, just before dusk. When we were almost on a level with the river it looked like itself, but when we were on the hillside above it, it looked like a long channel of quicksilver, lively but unmoving. Ben drove slow. Elmer followed us as far as Shorty's lane. We waved to him, Ben without turning his head, and he to us.

About a mile from the ranch, Ben pulled over—to piss, I thought at first.

"Don't feel good, son," he said. "It's all right." He leaned his crutches up against the trunk of a small tree, with one hand took hold of a branch that grew at about the height of his face, and leaned forward, bending his long body at the waist, like a hinge, and bending forward at the neck too, so that his face was far beyond his feet before he opened his mouth and began to vomit. He did it all neatly, like a man who knew how.

VIII

I wrote to Ben—not as soon as I should have—and finally in the winter we got a note back saying he'd had to give up the ranch. "I know you're not worried about the loan you were kind enough to make me, Myron, but I want you to know I haven't forgotten it." He was writing from McMinnville, Oregon, where his brother had a farm, and where he was going to stay "till I can leave," as he put it, and he said he would write at more length soon. "Maxie, gee the time flies even when it goes slow. You've started Junior High. When you get to college you can tell them you knew an old sixth-grade man once." And at the end, as if maybe he hadn't meant to, he mentioned Audrey and then went on and wrote more about her than anything else. She'd asked for a divorce, he said, and she was fine. She was on the road whenever the weather was good, successful with her donkey act, and she had a man-friend—"he travels to the same shows she does. I know him some, from the past, a fair kind of a bucking-horse rider. Young, but time and horses and women will cure that. I can't honestly say I'm over what I used to feel, but maybe I don't want to be. Anyhow, I wish her well."

I didn't write him back, and he didn't write again for a long time. His image in my mind began to fade. But two or three times, when I was walking down a city street and saw a tall, thin, rawboned man who was down-and-out or drunk or both, from a distance I thought it was Ben.

I was almost an adolescent now. If affections, taken together, have a shape, like a constellation, then the shape of mine in a short space of time had changed—or that was how it felt. Anna lived in the same house with me, but I hardly said a friendly word to her. Often I thought of my mother, but it wasn't she herself really that I remembered, but her illness, or details of it, like problems that keep coming back because you don't know how to solve them.

Sometimes when no one was around I'd go into my father's study, look at the papers on his desk, sit in his chair and swivel it around like I used to—though I was ashamed to do it now and considered myself too old.

On his desk were only things I thought uninteresting (so why did I go through them?): printed articles and abstracts, letters from political organizations asking for money, sheets of yellow paper covered with his handwriting in pencil. Mostly he didn't write in words but in mathematical symbols; some of them he formed so badly I couldn't tell what they were—and in any case didn't know what they meant, but I looked at them. The doodles that he made in the margins of the paper while he was thinking or daydreaming were drawn carefully: cubes, rhombohedrons, cylinders, cones. In each one he gave the illusion of a third dimension. I couldn't do it, so it impressed me; but even that I wouldn't admit.

One day (I had come home from school not long before; he was at his lab, I thought, and Anna at her office) I found a sheet of paper on top of the other papers, as if he'd just been writing on it. It had doodles on the side, and was written like a list, or with items on it like a list has, but some of them were crossed out.

—*Anna*

—*Kate's choice too*

—*Blessed us*

— ~~*Impossible not to deceive self*~~   *irrelevant*

—*Guilt, penalty partly of happiness*
   (of unhappiness too however)

—*Forgive self*

~~*(pleasant duty)*~~

It surprised me that he felt these things which I imagined were somehow akin to what I felt. When he and Anna talked about my mother in front of me, they usually talked about what she was like in the old days, things she had said and done before she was sick, and they'd ask me sometimes if I remembered. Sometimes I did, but without feeling, and I'd say, "No, I don't remember." I thought of that, and the good feeling I was starting to have went away, and I began to remember again the things I always remembered: My mother's body, on the bed, dressed in a blue dress, her hair brushed neatly back, her mouth still crooked, the dent in her forehead visible. She had had no right to be sick, and death had not made her well. I stared at my father's handwriting and remembered again how I had heard him call "Kate! Kate!" and I rushed in. But it was only a seizure. I had remembered it so many times, I didn't know why. After the seizure she was not much different from how she had been all the months before . . . but more listless. Suddenly, I remembered one morning when he had wheeled her into the kitchen. She wouldn't eat. It was not the first time . . . Maybe it wasn't any time, but all the times put together. No, it was one time, I remembered, it was in the morning. It must have been a Saturday, because Rose wasn't there, and I was. I was sitting at the kitchen table reading when he wheeled her in. He cut a small piece of casaba melon at the sideboard. I watched him put it on a plate. He tied a bib around her neck. He asked her if she would like a piece of melon. She said no, and he said: "But it's good! It won't be for long if we don't eat it." She looked up at him, shook her head, lowered it and closed her eyes. I kept on reading. He cut the slice of melon into pieces and set the plate on the wheelchair's wooden tray. He put a piece of melon on the fork and held it up. "Kate?" She looked up, took the bite into her mouth, chewed once or twice, swallowed, and shook her head. "Dear, won't you eat?" he said. There was a kind of agony in it for him. I saw that now, and some painful thought, some memory I didn't want to identify, came into my mind and went out again. She raised her head, I heard her voice, high and thin: "I'd like to be put down for my nap, Myron. Would you put me down for my nap, please?" and his: "But Kate, you just got up. Wouldn't you like to sit out in the garden?" She shook her head. He saw me looking at them. Remembering, I felt ashamed, and an instant later knew why: He had met my eyes and smiled, as if to say, "we're in this together," and I had looked away . . . My father appeared in the doorway. I was so startled my head jerked. I put the sheet of paper down. He walked over to me.

"Do you want to sit here?" I said.

"No, that's fine," he said.

"I don't need to," I said, getting up.

"That's true," he said, smiling. So we both stood. "I came across a list of Kate's medications. I'd forgotten how many of them there were." He picked up a typewritten sheet. "Here it is. I suppose it took me rather by surprise. Would you like to look at it?" "No." "Then I'll put it away somewhere. And what shall I do with this?" He picked up the sheet I had put down.

"Throw it out."

"Possibly . . . but we may be curious someday, about what thoughts were passing through our minds, years ago." He said

this too with a mild smile, and I just stared back at him, refusing
to alter the nonexpression on my face.

That night at supper I was silently rude, as usual more or less,
to him and to Anna. Afterwards, in my room, I read as late as I
could, afraid to relax my will, which was hardened against the
living and maybe the dead as well. Falling asleep I felt a sort of
brittle unpleasant excitement. Then, late at night, in the dark,
not knowing where I was but knowing I was on my feet in a
strange room with other people, shivering with fear, I heard myself call out—and my aunt call out, and then my father's voice
(gradually I realized I was in their bedroom) and felt his hands on
my shoulders.

The light came on. He was gone. I was standing near the
bed. My aunt, blinking, sat up partway. A spasm of shivers ran
through me. She moved to the bed's edge, put her feet on the
floor, reached out with her hand; her eyes, the pupils large and
dark, still blinking away sleep or darkness—but then my father
was there and she stopped. It passed through my mind, in a
strange remote way, as he was turning me away from her, that I
was naked and that if life were ever ordinary again, I would want
to make up then the shame I hadn't room inside to feel now.

My father steered me to the bathroom. Water was running in
the tub. He helped me lower myself into it. The warmth felt in-
stantly good. He sat down on the toilet seat and stayed there near
me, talking—the way he used to sit and talk while he bathed my
mother, to comfort her and himself, saying whatever came into
his head. Fear was like cold, he said to me now. It constricts the
blood vessels; and shivering is a violent reaction, a lively motion
meant to warm the body . . . but most people prefer a bath.
"*Body* is a strange word," I said, having said nothing else. He
laughed and asked what was strange about it. But I didn't know,
and didn't say any more, content just to feel weak and sleepy.

In the spring, Ben sent a note with a hundred-dollar bill folded into it.

Dear folks,

Hope you're all well. Wish I still had a place where you could all come and see me this summer. I've been living in tents, hotels—just anywhere they find to put us. Maybe I never told you, I'm working construction on the new inter-state highway that runs, or will run, between Yreka and Roseburg. Last fall I put my name in for a union shovel and came up lucky. Then on the job they found out I could run a bulldozer and I've been up on one ever since. Pays well, and it's good to have my feet back under me. Please find en-closed some of what I owe you, Myron.

Aside from that, not much is new. I'm keeping pretty dry on the inside. But on the outside, it rains enough to make a man shed tears, here, once it starts. I believe I may fly south, one day.

It had been more than a year and a half since we'd seen him when one short bright winter day he called my aunt at her office. He was in town, living in Culver City, at Sunset Stables. "Back to my old haunts," he said.

I opened the door before he knocked. He paused on the steps, holding his hat. "Well, old son, it's been a while."

"Not that long, though, hi," I said. We shook hands.

"It's been a growing spell for you."

"I know. Is your leg well?"

"Yes, sir, thanks."

We went through the house, out onto the porch. Not lame but a little stiff, thin, pale from having been up north so long, he stopped at the rail, put his hands on it and looked out. "I'd forgotten this view. There's our old stables. I said I'd look back at it someday, didn't know it'd be this soon." He turned and smiled at me. For a moment I felt the old passionate identification, fended it off and got sullen instead, though I tried not to show that, and pretty soon no longer felt too dangerously close to him, or resentful either.

"Did you get used to Oregon?"

"I did, but I never learned to like it."

"You made good money."

"That's right. I brought most of it back, couldn't find anything up there to spend it on." He touched his shirt pocket.

"My dad'll be here soon."

"I'll be glad to see him again."

"Would you like to sit down?"

He sat in the deck chair, still and composed, as if he could look out into the active world from some unmoving point inside himself. "You've grown so much I don't know if I know you."

"You do," I said.

He seemed to contemplate me for a minute, then he asked how Anna was.

With my face a mask, to show him that things were not as they used to be between me and her, between me and anyone, I said: "Fine."

He took this in and seemed to turn it over in his mind. "You're . . . thirteen now?"

"Fourteen, almost."

"Sure, you're older now, so you need a younger woman."

"No."

"No women at all, then?"

"Nope. None."

"None at all," he said and smiled a sort of half-smile. "I don't know, I don't think you've escaped yet."

I was both afraid and hoped that this was true, had begun to feel it, in my mind and in my glands, but I shook my head.

"You've got some misery coming," he said. "The girls will help you find it. It's sweet misery, too, a lot of it."

I blushed, and he took pity on me then and changed the subject. My aunt came through the open door. He stood up and held out his hand. She came forward past it and kissed him. My father came out too, and he and Ben shook hands. As soon as it was possible, Ben took the small thick white envelope with the money in it out of his shirt pocket. "I've brought this," he said. "Let's go count it out, in case I cheated one of us."

"Shall we go inside?"

"Where there's a table, that'd be fine," Ben said. "You come too, son, you can count higher than I can."

I took a step and stopped. "No, you go," I said. "It's between you."

"Really?" my father said.

I nodded.

"He's jumped the traces," Ben said.

From where the bus stopped you could see the long ramshackle barns, three or four of them. I stepped off; as I walked closer I saw the short barn branching off at right angles from one of the long ones. That should be his.

It was evening. The renthorse barns were closed to the public. A man and a woman and a girl my age were unsaddling and putting away the horses. Not asking or telling them anything, I walked by, feeling awkward—but they only looked at me.

The ground was like powder and rose in clouds, till I came to the place where the small barn branched off—here it was sprinkled and raked. I looked up and saw the thin smooth board, neatly painted, hanging down on wires from the eaves: Ben Webber / Horses Bought, Sold and Traded.

In amongst the hasp-latched stall doors, many of them with
horses looking out the upper half, I found an ordinary door with
a doorknob. I knocked and he opened it. "Come in, son. I'm almost ready, just let me change my shirt. Sit down, if you can find
something to sit on. Here, try this." It was a small wooden bar-
rel—a nailkeg—with a sheepskin tacked to the lid. The room itself was an old granary, half made-over. Windows had been cut
into it, but there was nothing to cook on, no bathroom, or even
a closet. Somebody had strung a doweling up across one corner,
and a few of Ben's pressed shirts with cleaner's tags on them hung
on hangers from that. And there was a wagonwheel suspended
from the ceiling as a chandelier, with electrical cord wrapped
around three of the spokes and bulbs hanging down. He'd been
here a few weeks already, but his trunk—which was almost all he
had in the world besides his old green Plymouth, a horse trailer,
some horses he'd bought recently and a fair amount of cash—was
only partly unpacked. "It's a bachelor life here for sure," he said,
as he saw me looking around. But why he should have so few pos-
sessions, when he'd had a whole household eighteen months
ago, was something I didn't have experience enough to wonder
clearly about. In fact to me it seemed fitting, for a new start in the
world. It was years later, in bits and pieces, that he told me. The
hardest thing for him to talk about—harder than Audrey had
ever been—was the way he'd gone about leaving the ranch. Parts
of it—fighting like a sick dog with his brother's sons when they'd
loaded him into the backseat of his own car; and cursing out Elmer for interfering in what wasn't his business—those parts he
had no clear memory of. And other parts—Elmer finding him
passed out over his own table, with the cow unmilked, and the
house smelling of whiskey and garbage—he'd never remembered at all. They took him to Oregon. It was Elmer who had
called his brother. It was Elmer who settled things up for him and
sent him a check—sold all he could at auction in Modesto. And

Ben had written him later, when he was dry, and thanked him for everything. Yet he never got over it really; he got almost over everything else, but not the shame he felt from that, and some resentment too, which added to the shame, because there was nothing he had a right to resent.

His horse trailer was already hitched to the car. We got in and took off. As we drove along he told me he was on the lookout for a stables of his own, like he'd had before. Meanwhile he was putting together a string of horses so he'd be ready to set up business when he found one.

"Do you like the stables business now?" I said.

"No," he said. "I'll make money at it, though, I think. I did before."

And after that? I didn't ask and he didn't say. He was an open-natured man as always, but he'd grown cautious and didn't put words to his hopes anymore, beyond the immediate future.

On our way, or more likely it was a mile or so out of the way and I didn't notice, we came to a plain square building on a street corner, white in the dusk: Mashburn Brothers Market. He slowed down, way down almost to a stop, so that cars had to move around us. "That's where I do my shopping now."

"I don't mind if you want to stop and get something."

"I don't want anything I can get very easy," he said, by which I had a sort of half-idea what he meant, or at least that he meant something.

"Do you know somebody there?"

"Not as well as I'd like to," he said. "Well, let's go on." And he sped up. "I know Oscar Mashburn. I knew his brother too, before he died."

"And—?"

"You mean that won't do? Her name's Gladys."

"What does she do?"

"She works there."

"Have you taken her out?"

"No, sir. I haven't asked her. She might not go. I said to Oscar the other day, after she'd waited on me about three, four times: 'Who's your new checker?' 'Where?' he said, like he didn't know he had one. 'Right there,' I said, 'the good-looking one, with a lilt in her voice—where's she from?' And he said: 'Why, that's my sister-in-law. You know her. She's been around for years. If you haven't met her, come over here and meet her.' So I met her. She calls me Mr. Webber now, every time I go through the line, which is about four times a week. I have a lot of shopping to do . . . I saw an old friend of yours too, yesterday."

"Audrey?"

"She's wintering here in the city."

"Where did you see her?"

"Right where I live. Sunset Stables."

"She came to see you?"

"She didn't know I was even in town. She was bringing her friend, to show him her old stomping grounds. They might be here tonight too, at the sale. He's shopping for some calves."

"You talk about her so calmly."

"Well, I'm making an effort."

"When you used to make an effort, it didn't work."

"There's truth in that," he said. "I've got some ballast now."

"Can I have some?"

"Not of mine . . . That's the first time I ever heard you make a joke. I guess it was a joke."

"I guess."

We were walking across the dark lot toward the lighted door of the auction barn. Other people, shadowy like us, were converging on it too, and others were coming out. The cattle were done selling, and horses were about to start.

"Look here!" Ben said softly. I looked up and saw two figures, male and female, coming toward us. "Did you get your calves bought?" Ben said in a loud voice, meant to be friendly. Her boyfriend said: "Me?" and she said: "Ben?" "Sure enough," he said. Then they were close enough to see our faces and she said: "And you?—Gosh! it's you." She didn't hug me this time, because she couldn't hug Ben, but she shook my hand, and then we all shook each other's hands.

It was awkward. "Stop by, when you're down at the fairgrounds," the boyfriend said. "Remember I told you, I'm parked down at the east end: blue-and-white trailer." "You bet. I'll try," Ben said. And they shook hands again.

But it was brief. Once or twice in the dim light I'd seen her face, but noticed only that she smiled at me, and measured me with her eyes because I'd grown.

"Audrey's happy," he said as we walked on. "It shows in her face whether she wants it to or not—just like the unhappiness used to."

"It's good that she is," I said.

"If we wish her well, sure," he said.

"I do," I said. "So do you."

"I try," he said, and after we walked a little farther: "How about Anna?" he said. "You think she's happy?"

"Yes."

"I guess we have to wish her well too, then."

I didn't answer. We went through the door into the crowd and the light and up into the stands.

Ben bid on half a dozen horses during the night. One he bought, and he was satisfied: a gentle, reliable gelding, old and settled in his ways. By eleven o'clock the sale was still going on, but he said it was about time to go, and I was ready. The bench was hard, and the air was full of smoke, and the smoke and dust and bright light stung my eyes because I was already sleepy. Then a girl rode one of the horses into the ring, riding him bareback to show how gentle he was, and with no bridle on him or even a halter, just a piece of orange baling-twine looped around his neck to guide him with. Her hair was long and brown and she wore it pulled back in a single braid. She was fourteen or fifteen. I looked around at Ben, but he was yawning. She was nothing to him, and the things he'd said, which kept rolling around in my mind, were gone from his: that I needed ballast to help me wish Anna well, which I had to do because she was happy, and that my time of sweet misery was coming. She jogged the horse from one side of the ring to the other, set him up sharp and turned him hard, with the twine and with her knees and little clicks from her tongue. I felt a kind of pleasant confusion. At the same time, it wasn't really pleasant to be confused. I didn't know what I felt, or what caused it. It wasn't her body exactly. Underneath the jacket and the chaps that she wore, I could hardly tell where her body was. Her face I could see, but the feeling itself somehow made her face so indistinct that I didn't know if I would know it again, even in ten minutes. It was motion most of all: the motion of her braid swinging, the motion of her bobbing head, of her back and arms, of her legs pressing against the moving sides of the horse. It was as if all motion, the horse's too, were hers. The horse stopped. She fell forward a little, reached down with her hand to balance herself, and her fingers took hold of the horse's mane . . . The bidding started. In the background, far back, making its way as if through cotton, I heard Ben's voice.

"Well, should we call it a night?" I turned by an effort. He saw my face and kept back the bigger part of a smile. "There's no hurry," he said. "I didn't know you were busy."

Design by David Bullen
Typeset in Mergenthaler Goudy Olde Style
with Perpetua display
by Wilsted & Taylor
Printed by Maple-Vail
on acid-free paper